THE MATTRESS TURNER

OF

TWIGMERE

Rebecca J. Cunningham

Published by BLUJAH BOOKS 2017

blujah. co.uk
blujah.books@gmail
First published in Great Britain 2017
ISBN: 9780954261658

Printed and bound in Great Britain by
Witley Press Ltd
24-26, Greevegate,
Hunstanton
PE366AD

Cover design by **Abi Daker**
Impression number 1

THE MATTRESS TURNER

OF

TWIGMERE

Rebecca J. Cunningham

A SUPERNATURAL WHIMSY

For
The Illustrious
Mr. Frederick William Cunningham,
Actor
And those who stand beside

1858
London

An Introduction & a Lady is Amused

The gentleman, attired in black frock coat, silk top hat in hand, was ushered into the room by the equerry and left there without introduction.

It was a large room, gravely decorated, heavily curtained and silent except for the busy scratching of a pen on paper, which occupied the figure seated at the desk.

The man gave a low bow. 'Ma'am.'

The figure turned, causing a gentle ripple in the flounces of her morning dress. She frowned and resumed her business. 'You have come for the lifting, Mr – '

'Purse. Mr. Humphrey Purse,' intoned the man softly and he bowed again.

The visitor could not be certain, but from where he stood, thought he observed the slightest flicker of mirth lighten the woman's severe demeanour.

'Mr. Humphrey Purse, I am certain that we may oblige you with directions.' And with an almost imperceptible movement of her arm, she plucked a bell from her desk and rang it.

Once more, the man bowed, noting on his slow

journey up that the short, matronly woman now standing before him was wearing an expression of naked surprise.

'Mr. Purse, with the greatest respect, I cannot begin to imagine how a man of your age could possibly undertake such a strenuous task. Have you an assistant?'

'Thank you, Ma'am, for your concern. Allow me to put your mind at ease. I have no need of an assistant. I find that my strength, even with the advancement of years, is sufficient to effect the task I put at your pleasure. Indeed, if I may be so bold as to advise that in this esteemed instance it is a mere matter of *adjustments*.'

The woman acknowledged these words with a nod, tiny creases trembling at the sides of her mouth. She was not handsome, yet her sudden playfulness lent an attractive colour to otherwise plain features. 'Mr. Purse, I look forward to the benefits of the "adjustments". I trust they will be faithful to the promises you describe in your many interesting letters.'

Even if it were proper, which it was not, there was no time for reply. A rap on the door summoned Mr. Humphrey Purse. He withdrew graciously and followed the servant to a private chamber.

Nowabouts
Twigmere

A Beginning for Some
An Ancient Dwelling in Twigmere

Placing five pairs of spectacles on the small table before him, Mr. Gifford Hans leaned back in his chair and considered the array. The spectacles were each of a different colour, shape and varying strength of lens.

The old man subscribed to the notion that eyes should not be encouraged to laziness, and that a little exercise is far less injurious to sight than a dependency upon ever-increasing magnification.

Mr. Hans selected a pair from the small pile and slotted them upon the bridge of his well-shaped nose. He turned his head from side to side, peering through the tiny pinholes in the black moulded plastic. Lifting a letter from the table, he leaned closer and found that, with a little focus, the words were just discernible. The ancient removed the spectacles, replacing them with a pair of thick lenses set in pink National Health frames and continued perusing the letter.

Because of the surname, perhaps, Mr. Hans was often taken to be of German or Austrian extraction, yet those clients on meeting the bright, unblinking blue eyes behind whatever day's glasses he wore, discovered that he was as English as acorns.

He lived in an old terraced cottage in Twigmere, Surrey's most southerly town. No one knew when he'd moved there, because successive buyers of neighbouring property had been inheriting 'the very quiet gentleman next door' for decades.

Twigmere, with its population of 20,000 souls, was served by excellent communications. At one time, the town boasted the highest number of first-class rail ticket holders within the south-east – a fact much lauded by local estate agents and those newly mortgaged to its delights.

At first sight, it was indeed a delightful and comfortable manor. Narrow, curling streets led to a modest shopping centre, a decent museum, an AGA outlet and a well-respected supermarket. A little beyond the centre, examples of the worthy Arts & Crafts movement were beaded amongst Edwardian and Victorian dwellings. On sunny afternoons, with a mellow sun threaded along rustic roofs, the place was becalmed in quietude and residential integrity. Its hedgerows were shapely, its gardens careful and the views from nearby elevations spectacular. Altogether, the place appeared to own the genteel restraint of a Methodist's jumble sale.

There were, naturally, pockets of discontent, grumblings at the folly of town planners, the avarice of developers and the Johnnies-come-lately traducing the subtle customs of Twigmere's oldest denizens.

Mr. G. Hans may well have begun to share such concerns, or maybe he'd always known of them. Folding the letter he'd been reading, he slotted it in between Wednesday's and Thursday's spectacles, and sighed.

2014
Surrey

Lydia Jellow
Travels of a Capacious Bag
&
A Silver-Topped Walking Stick

In a bedding store opposite Twigmere's finest hotel, a customer prodded the polythene-encased stock beneath the encouraging gaze of the young manager, Ben Glee. 'Please, do try, madam.'

The middle-aged, twice divorced, once widowed woman lumped herself onto the bed, hauled up her oversized handbag and lay staring at the ceiling's ornate coving. The bed was okay. Firm, but that's the least you'd expect. She wasn't convinced it would be the amazing, transforming experience the brochure promised. Rolling off the bed, the bag's leather strap now looped on her arm, she stood by the side and slid her fingers between the mattress's slippery sheath and its divan cover of gingham ticking.

'Christ-all-bloody-mighty.' Not to be beaten, she dropped her possessions to the shop floor, prised both hands beneath the mattress and attempted to lever up the side. It wouldn't budge. 'What's in there, dead bodies?'

'Hand-coiled springs, horsetails – '

'Horse what?'

'And wool, madam. The top-end products do have cashmere – and, of course, flax to keep the bed completely silent.'

'As the grave after the coronary you get trying to lift the thing.'

'We do provide a mattress-turning service,' the young man said, surprisingly. 'For a small fee we have someone to assist with the lifting. If you so wish.'

'Eh?'

This unique and exclusive aftercare service for Glee's more discerning customer was far from new; Ben's father also briefly used a man. In fact, from recently bequeathed records, Ben discovered this facility had discreetly endured, on and off, since the shop had been in existence – over one and-a-half centuries. And when he saw the prospective customer struggling with a hefty, hand-coiled affair, he announced the offer with an assurance born of ancient habit.

The customer arched a pair of tinted eyebrows, an uncertain smile working through her crimson lips. 'You actually *employ* someone to turn mattresses?'

'Ones that are purchased from us,' he qualified, gravely.

'And how small is this fee?'

'In the region of seventy pounds, for each visit.'

The woman folded her arms, mouth now fixed at the 'don't give me that' slant.

Ben smiled, his easy face lighting good-naturedly. 'Just an option, madam, but as you've discovered, a mattress of this quality can be very unwieldy. So that you may enjoy the full benefit of the product, we do recommend turning on a regular basis.'

'Regular?'

'We advise seasonally.'

'Soon adds up.' The customer's attention wandered over the top of Ben's neatly parted hair, myriad thoughts sifting through her busy mind. She was secretly captivated by the notion of having a bed operative – no one she knew was privy to such a thing. 'How far out does he go, this mattress guy?'

'I don't believe Mr. Hans has ever specified a radius. Distance has never been discussed.'

'Could the fee or whatever be included for a couple of years?' The woman caressed the mattress's polythene cover. 'As I'm paying cash, you could have a word with your boss.'

It was Ben's turn to raise an eyebrow. 'I am the boss, madam. And that would not be possible.' He hesitated, as though encountering the fact for the first time. 'We prefer to keep our accounts separate,' he said, adding archly, 'Mr. Hans is much in demand and often booked up well in advance with our established patrons.'

The prospect of hiring a 'man to turn' was piqued by this notion of selectivity – quite a thing, being a patron. She scanned the manager's name badge. 'Okay, Ben, *ambassador,* you've convinced me. I'll take the bed.'

'You've made an excellent choice, madam.'

'Do I get it signed?'

'I believe with certain products there is indeed a signature.'

The woman rolled her eyes.

'I can find out for you, madam.'

'Don't bother, but I'll definitely need this Hans mattress character.'

'I'll certainly add your name to his list.'

The customer wasn't doing too well in the personalised treatment department, and lists involved waiting for others to go first. Still, there was that added frisson, the possibility of jumping ahead – in an emergency. 'And pop me on the list.'

'May I take a name?'

'Jellow.'

An address was provided and a substantial deposit reluctantly given.

Mrs. Jellow left Glee's Bedding, 'ambassadors to the most exclusive beds in the land', not convinced she'd secured the quaint services of a man called Hans, but with the chilling certainty that a North West London company was expecting the balance of six thousand, three hundred pounds to be paid no later than two months before delivery.

Outside on a bench next to a cross honouring the town's dead of two world wars, Lydia sucked in long draughts of damp January air. She became vaguely aware of a tall elderly man, a silver-topped walking stick in hand, lowering himself slowly beside her. Instinctively, as a mother might draw her infant from danger, she swept up that capacious bag and hugged it to her chest. Looking across the road to a little café, she wondered if anyone in Twigmere could afford to eat.

More of an Ancient, Dwelling in Twigmere

Mr. Hans preferred to sleep downstairs in his small cottage. He found the upper floor afforded him the clarity required for research and special investigations. Below, on the other hand, in the muddle of his sleeping quarters and with a window facing directly onto the pavement, he found perverse relaxation in the distraction of traffic and human bustle.

Missive in hand, a pair of pink glasses perched on the bridge of his nose, he made his way upstairs. Four wooden filing cabinets were cramped in the far corner of a dim, dusty room. He pottered over to the cabinet closest to the window and slid out a drawer marked I-L. In the sudden rush of air, a strip of damp wallpaper flapped down and curled above the gaping darkness.

With the dexterity of a concert pianist, his bone-white fingers rippled frantically across the open drawer's invisible contents. A shimmering spider's web of evening sun spun across the filthy windowpane as he closed in on his prey. At last, with a triumphal smile, he produced a small, buff-coloured card containing handwritten details of a date, time and address. He gave the card a little flourish and then checked it briefly against the letter. Closing the filing cabinet drawer, he pressed the wallpaper back to its position and creaked back down to his bedroom.

Returned to his seat, he straightened his burgundy and green check suit and settled down to re-examine the contents of the letter. He gave a sudden cluck of disapproval and swept the pink spectacles off, dangling them aloft.

In the distance, the Town Hall bell sounded the hour. The light was fading and a tenebrous gloom cloaked the small room.

He stretched up and moved to the fireplace in the corner, sealed in grey contemplation. Some minutes passed before he stirred, then, lifting a wooden clock from the mantelpiece, he felt at the back for its key and turned the cool metal, and again, until the machine began to tick. Slow and sullen, as if torn from the refuge of slumber, the clock's mechanics dragged themselves into rhythmic life, and then fell silent. The old man shook the thing, opened its glass face and moved the hands around until it said ten minutes past seven and returned it to the iron shelf with a bang. 'That will do.' Reaching into his pocket, he fetched out a box of matches and put light to some letters in the grate.

At his bed, a crude, institutional issue, he flipped back the sheet and sat, his head bowed.

An angry crackling burst of light from the hearth cast the room into a luminous, triangular form. The fire, having devoured what little fuel there was, licked around the chimney and then coiled in a spiralling, greedy flame, finally withering to ash.

The place would have been engulfed in deepest night, save for a small pool of green translucent light eddying around the clock face and across Mr. Hans as he lay, corpse-like, upon his bed.

1910
Twigmere

Jacob
Slipping the Reins

As the Town Hall clock struck nine, Mr. Jacob Glee, round and bewhiskered, hooked a long pole onto the awning of his shop. Slowly and showing little enthusiasm, he tugged out the canvas until the faded blue of *Glee's of Twigmere* was visible. Pole by his side, he surveyed the empty street as if expecting someone to appear, and then stepped back into the shop.

Inside, his wife was busy at a mahogany washstand, thumbing a beeswax cloth into its delicate marquetry. 'We got that delivery of chairs in at last,' she said, with a warm smile.

He slotted the pole in its place behind the shop door. 'Should stay fine, Minnie. I'll bring 'em out later. Got to attend to these ruddy new mattresses first.'

'Righty-o. When our Benjamin arrives, he can give you a hand. Don't forget it's half day, Mr. Glee. You did promise a little trip to the Isle of Wight to see what they done to that house.'

Jacob nodded and lifted a forlorn gaze ceilingwards. 'Do you realise, Mrs. Glee, that our dear Queen has been gone near on ten years?'

She shook her head. 'Time don't wait and neither do customers. Now off with you, my love.'

He wiped his hands on his apron, collected a

purchase book from his desk and mounted the few steps to a mezzanine floor.

Dropping the book on a chair, he clicked on a torch and angled its weak light over the room. Four thick pocket-coiled spring mattresses leaned heavily against the wall. 'Deep and firm as a well-upholstered settee', as one high-class periodical had promised. Sentried opposite, lovingly polished brass bedsteads glowered at their usurpers.

There was no demand for proper beds these days. What was wrong with the flock, or feather overlays, soft, comfortable and easy to move? Jacob thought. He couldn't put his mind to selling these monstrosities that needed two men to lift.

He tugged at the wax tape slung around his neck, but instead of measuring up the new stock, he moved the torch to the corner, where a box file had been carefully hidden. He crouched down and began rummaging among its contents, senses alert to any ascending footsteps.

After a short while, Minnie's voice drifted from the shop. 'Are you all right up there? You gone very quiet.'

A frown disturbed Jacob's passive features. He craned around, his voice steering its soothing tones. 'Won't be long.'

'I don't trust that new floor without no light. You could trip, my love.'

'It's safe as houses, Minnie.' His eyes suddenly itched and for a second he couldn't see. Blinking away the dust, he picked up the purchase book and checked the order, giving a quick glance over to the bases.

There was no need to measure. Jacob knew perfectly well they wouldn't fit, and whipped off the tape. 'Minnie!'

Mrs. Glee, as stout and padded as a settee herself, took a few wary steps to join her husband.

'These ain't right,' he said, waving the tape and pointing to some figures in the open order book.

'Oh dear, not again. And here comes our Benjamin.'

A tall, foppish man twiddling a fashionable American cane swaggered onto the shop floor and peered around. 'Anyone in attendance?' Rattling his cane across the newly delivered chairs, he paced towards the mezzanine and called up. 'I see you got the brown furniture in again, Pop. What have I been telling you?'

Jacob leaned over, and beckoned to his son. 'Them new mattresses be too big for my frames. They're no good; we'll have to send 'em back.'

Benjamin climbed the steps and cast a casual eye over the offending items. 'That ain't a clever idea, Pop. You'll lose on 'em and never make it up. I reckon it's your frames what need to go.' He tapped his finger against a gleaming finial. 'They don't want these brass things no more, not with all that cleaning. And with new houses coming we're bound to get more select folks coming in.'

'We've kept our customers years. And they're select enough.'

'Yes, Pop. Same ones we had since Grandpa Benjamin. Folks expect us to be like London now, with modern stock. Plus all electric lighting. We got to get ahead, that's what he would've wanted.'

Minnie folded her arms. 'I never heard such talk.'

'He's right, Mother.' Jacob placed a reassuring hand on his wife's arm, mood warmed by a returning idea. 'I been too old and stubborn to see it. His grandpa would expect nothing less than that.'

The formidably energetic Benjamin Horace Glee, a man of considerable personality had, by foul means and fair, been getting ahead for fifty long years. He'd waited until his late nineties before reluctantly passing the shop over to his son, Jacob.

Now, with the old tyrant's recent death at the remarkable, if inconsiderate, age of one hundred and two, the beleaguered offspring was looking forward to a modicum of peace. For truth be told, with his sentimental love of the old Queen and passion for the railways, Jacob was never cut out to be a proprietor, of this, or any other establishment.

His own son, however, shared no such misgivings about business or the modern manner by which it came. Like his namesake, young Benjamin was raw, enterprising and, by some mystical twist of fate, was the image of him, too.

Time for Jacob to slip the reins and pass Glee's of Twigmere to the young scion. An enthusiastic and able pair of hands, who would, on the instant he became proprietor, commission a signwriter to adorn the name *'Glee & Sons. Purveyors of Fine Beds and Furnishings'* on the store's large, shiny window. A while afterwards, *'Other Services Rendered',* added in discreet lettering beneath.

2014

Lydia Wakes

Mrs. Jellow regretted her purchase the moment she set foot on the train back to London, as if by the very act of leaving Twigmere, reality had struck and stunned her from the town's mesmerising vapours.

She stared through the window like a sobering drunk forced to confront actions borne of intoxication. 'I cannot believe I have just spent seven thousand quid on a fucking bed. I've been hypnotised.' She narrowed her eyes and squinted at a distant possibility. 'That's assault.'

The hangover of horror persisted throughout her journey to Waterloo. On the crowded Northern Line platform, she sagged miserably behind a thicket of commuters, plotting ways to cancel the process, without losing her considerable deposit and pride to match.

When the train arrived, she pummelled her way to a seat and sank down, crushed with exhaustion. Opening her cavernous bag, she wearily plotted its contents and drew out the receipt.

Apparently, the bed would take months to make. Plenty of time to invent a death in the family: the aged relative, for whom she had so generously purchased the item, had now clogged it. Anyway, the company must be insured against people coming to their senses; mind changing must be happening on a daily basis in that hideously overvalued trade. Let's face it, affluent

Londoners know a scam when they see one; they just pretend to go along with it. She looked at the receipt again, and saw the company address. 'My God,' she muttered. 'It's got a Tube station.'

Yet the effects of that strange bewitchment enjoyed something of a second wind. By the time Lydia arrived home, she'd changed her mind about cancelling, that abundant imagination plugging any gaps in credulity. Friends were informed of her cosmically amazing discovery in deepest Surrey, where she'd been fitted for a bespoke service that was 'Literally Out Of This World.' And in the hope that it may make them jealous, refused to tell them exactly where or what it was.

That was several months ago, and her letter, folded inside Ben Glee's neatly written recommendation of a new client, had been duly noted.

Autumn 2014
Twickenham, Middlesex

Prunella
Falling, The Anatomy of a Spoon
&
A Case of Attribution

It was a fine Sunday in mid autumn. Fallen leaves curled and snapped beneath the tread of locals enjoying an afternoon on their 'village green'.

A pale, slight figure adorned in chiffon gown shimmered into view and began to dance. Her actions, observed by these locals, did not seem to rouse concern, as though a singular woman performing ballet sequences on that sacred ground was perfectly usual.

As she pirouetted, her headdress of gauze feathers fluttered loose and then took flight. On she danced, her toe points stippling the ground so fast she seem to float above it. Suddenly, she leapt toward the iron bridge that crossed a small river, twirling and whirling, and offered a supple arabesque to the mellow sky. Then back, those tiny steps skimming the earth before coming to a halt at a great copper beech. Here, the dancer arched her spine, extending her quivering arms to their mournful reach and then, from one supernatural fist of energy, performed her *grande jeté* across a stage of broken leaves.

She sank to the ground, and lay perfectly still.

A few days before her dramatic finale in the local park, ninety eight year old (or thereabouts) Prunella Flaggon summoned her granddaughter, Sophie to supper.

The preamble to the meal had been without incident. Prunella, having made casual enquiry of her granddaughter's well-being, and Sophie offering a sullen 'okay', they'd both seated themselves at the table.

A thin flame from an oil lamp sputtered, creating more spectral shadow than illumination. The place reeked of paraffin.

Deftly unplugging a bottle of Sauvignon Blanc, Sophie filled two large crystal glasses and slid one towards her grandmother. 'Bit dark in here.'

Resplendent in silk turban and lilac duster coat, the grandmother reached for her soup spoon. 'It offers a moment for reflection in these times of gratuitous liberalism,' she said.

Sophie took two long gulps of wine. 'I thought you were into that, you know, liberal thing.'

'For myself, of course. Others simply do not know where to stop.'

The granddaughter topped up her drink and searched around for a distraction.

'The world has become far too queer, you know,' the grandmother continued.

'*Gay*, you mean?'

'As you wish. However, I do believe the throwback is enjoying an ironic revival. The North London *agonati* love to own a denigration. Mostly on behalf of those who are either dead, or past caring.' She pointed her silver spoon at Sophie, its rat-tail stem balanced in the ancient grip. 'Let me tell you, homosexuals were far more entertaining when they were the scourge of society. This 'coming out' has made them intolerant and completely without humour.'

Sophie didn't have an answer to that.

'And no one complains of their taste in cross-dressing, which is to say the least, appalling,' she rattled on, soup still unsipped. 'And how long must we endure the spectacle of the dart-playing female with the gait of a Welsh miner, without recourse to comment?'

'There aren't Welsh miners anymore, Granny.'

'I don't care if it's a career lesbian with their best pantomime swagger, they are all utterly without aesthetic recommendation.' She considered for a moment, eyes bright with genuine enquiry. 'Are you a *gay*, dear?'

The granddaughter shook her head, and fished out a strand of mousey hair from her wine glass.

'Just as well – if you have the option, my dear. And it does seem that every orientation is compelled to reproduce, via whatever method and no matter how ungainly.'

Sophie's blush went unnoticed in that sepulchral gloom, her mind shaping a guilty quest.

'Mind you, all that's old hat,' the mordant crone observed. 'When I remember those sperm-hunting women at Hebden Bridge, my blood runs cold. Northern men used and then flung aside, along with pedigree.' Her brow tightened, plucked in papery folds. 'Where are those fatherless children now?'

Sophie gaped in astonishment. 'Well, there's me.'

'Your father doesn't count. So bland, he was worse than useless. Anyway, it was he who ran to the other side of the world.'

'And Grandpa. What about him?' Sophie reminded her, with tremulous indignation.

'Your mother met him, at least.'

'So how's him being flung away different from someone deciding to do it on their own now?'

Prunella watched with searing eyes.

The granddaughter rustled in her bag. 'I can't see how that's different,' she said loudly, over the emergence of another bottle. 'If someone's like *really* desperate for a baby and there's no one around, permanent, or whatever, does it matter?' She unscrewed the wine top and sat, small metal cap in one hand, large bottle in the other, as if demonstrating the overwhelming weight of reason. 'I just think it's nice.'

'*Nice*?' The old woman lowered the spoon, its baroque shoulders meeting the rim of her dish with a sound clunk. 'The unborn will not thank you for snatching them from oblivion, especially by someone who can barely remain conscious herself.'

Sophie bit her quivering lip, a tide of injustice rising. 'You did, and it turned out like that anyway with Mum. People share now. It's different.' She stabbed her brimming gaze around the room. 'I don't want to end up like you, on my own all the time. You are actually a lonely old woman, Granny.'

Prunella creased back in her chair, fronds of turban unfurling in the ghostly light. 'And producing makes us less alone? I can assure you, children will find you out. Foibles and terrors incubated for generations are merely transferred to the wretched offspring, and there you are. Again.'

'What's that supposed to mean?'

'Life is a supermarket, as far as you're concerned. A series of aisles to distract. Grabbing this and that to fill a void.'

'So? And how about you? You know, with everything you did. That's the reason Mum hates you. You do know that she does actually hate you?''

The ancient didn't flinch.

'No one comes here, Granny,' she pointed out, voice choking on audacity. 'I'm the only one who bothers. If it wasn't for me, you'd never have visitors at all. Absolutely nobody.'

'Bravo!' Prunella raised her glass. 'I'm certain they will arrive, when the time is ripe,' she said, offering a dazzling smile. 'And remember, we only need the one. *Bon appétit.*'

2014

Lydia

What a Card

In the intervening months since her visit to Twigmere, Lydia Jellow moved house. She'd informed Glee's of her new address, suggesting that Mr. Hans contact her personally to make an appointment.

Ben didn't pass that element of the message on to the mattress turner; there was simply no point. He merely sent a brief handwritten note informing him of the change of details.

When Ben checked the appointment diary, he found Mrs. Jellow's new address crossed out and her old one in its stead, along with a few others he did not recognise.

As with most of her decisions, Lydia's move was sudden. Apart from anything else, property values in London had soared so high it seemed an insult to capitalism not to cash in.

The divorcee-cum-widow had done ludicrously well over the years from the sales of her 'settlement/probate' properties. Her most recent cashing in had enabled her to purchase a small cottage outright in a sought-after Hertfordshire town.

All her debts were paid off, including the purchase from Glee's. And, by pointing out what looked suspiciously like a speck of crimson lipstick on a set of superb linen, she'd got a substantial discount in that highly regarded store.

Mrs. Jellow liked to get the better deal. Ex- and dead husband-wise, she generally did.

She'd researched the small company in North West London, discovering that the manufacturers, or '*bespoke sleep makers*', supplied beds and mattress to celebrities and other modern aristocracy. Scrutinising their latest brochure, it became apparent that her purchase was at the low-end range, and that most beds sold for several thousands above what she'd paid.

'Eighty grand? They need their heads examining.'

To secure maximum exposure in her new self-regarding and precious locale, she'd arranged the delivery for a Saturday a.m. slot. There would, she imagined, be witnesses to her excellent taste, as per lettering on a van painted in the company's own brand of muted Dickensian. What would be the slogan? '*Exclusive hand-crafted beds*' or '*Luxury bed-makers to royalty*', with a royal coat of arms, perhaps? Ever-watchful neighbours would look that up to make sure and realise that newcomer Lydia Jellow was kosher.

That morning she'd re-tidied the house, hid the futon in the downstairs cupboard and made certain that her bedroom was ready for the new addition. In the front room, she flopped back onto a long sofa and glanced at the clock – it was only ten. Yesterday's letter from Glee's was still on the armrest. It was an odd, old-fashioned communication, trusting in her delight at finally receiving her order, which they confirmed to be at eleven on the day in question. Unusual for a firm to bother with such niceties. Folding the note back into its envelope, her finger touched the sharp edge of something she'd missed, small and smooth. Swinging her legs up on the cushions, Lydia, puckered open the envelope and slid out a business card. Elegant, pure-white lettering set against a deep burgundy background read: *Gifford Hans. Mattress Turner* and just below this, in small copperplate: *A Personal Service for the Promotion of Perfect Sleep.* Nothing else – no address, email or phone number. 'Eh? Weird.' She stood and crossed to the window, card still in hand.

She was surprised to see a battered blue Luton van trundling noisily up and down the cul-de-sac. It juddered to an untidy halt outside her house. *Bob's Great Mover's* was daubed in yellow on the vehicle's dented side and a telephone number scratched beneath. Vaguely contemplating the extra apostrophe, Lydia dismissed the vision as a wrong turning for a council estate, and returned to the sofa.

The doorknocker summoned her in a thundering tattoo, followed by what sounded like fists pounding the wood. On the step, she found two sullen and unshaven men glaring up at her. The one with the keys, driver, she presumed, said, 'We got bed. Deliver bed.' He jerked his head toward the Luton. 'Okay. We get now. Good.' He marched away in the direction of the parked van. His companion scowled accusingly past Lydia to the narrow hallway, cursing in a language she couldn't understand, before joining his mate.

She felt weak with shame and sloped into the front room. Could you believe it? The company spent all this bollocks on the high-end product, the bespoke mattress and then sent gangsters and people smugglers to deliver it. Outrage bourgeoned among her bitter tears. 'I hope to God no one's died in that van. I'll give the bastards smarmy letters.' And she gave the sofa a violent kick.

Meanwhile, the men grunted and thumped. 'Lady, where you want?'

They had only reached the hallway.

'I was thinking upstairs. In the bedroom.'

The companion grimaced and shook his head in disgust.

'Oh, for God's sake, what's the matter with you? Do you know how much that bloody thing cost?'

'We no speak English, lady. Heavy. After, maybe bed no good.' And the men commenced shoving the brute to the bedroom.

Mrs. Jellow charted the trail of chaos up the stairs and entered the room to find the men cross-legged on the floor. The anthropomorphic mattress, still encased in its plastic guard, leaned fatly defiant against the far wall like a thuggish squatter. By all accounts it should have suffocated, but the chances were it was made of stuff that would never die.

'What about the base? The divan's got to come up. Where is it?' Lydia heard herself squeak, panic rising. 'For crying-out-fucking-loud. I hope the idiot who sent you cabbage picking clowns put everything on the van.'

The driver affected shock and mopped his dry brow with a censorious hand.

Lydia said, 'Don't give me that. You better get the rest of it, or else I will be tipping you in bloody zlotys.'

At this, both men sprang to their feet, thumping their chests in pain at the insult. 'Not Polish. No, lady, we not Polish. Bulgarian, my friend he the Ukraine. Good men. We get. No zlotys.'

When it was over, she surveyed the result of all this effort. It wasn't what she expected at all: the bed was too tall, imposing. It bullied away the room's original features, so meticulously and expensively restored.

Lydia felt suddenly vulnerable, once more overcome with tears. Lifting an old Welsh blanket from a side chair, she spread it across the mattress and clambered on top, resting her damp face on the coarse weave. The stairs creaked, old oak popping, recovering from the recent onslaught, most likely. She turned her head to the open door and was surprised to see how different everything appeared: the window, the view of the stairs and the landing, all seen from a different perspective – as if from afar. Closing her eyes, she thought of the shop in Twigmere, the funny manager there, with his squeaky voice. You honestly couldn't bear him a grudge, or those men, refugees probably forced to work for a mafia boss and sleep in that dodgy van. Her softening thoughts meandered onto the mattress turner himself. Yes, him – she still had his card in her hand. She must find out about this Mr. Gifford Hans. He'd know why she felt so weird.

2014

The Properties of a Lady & Miscellaneous Items

In the deceased's Twickenham flat, a space crammed with decades of saleroom purchases, guests mingled uneasily, pouring their own drinks and thinking up decent things to say.

Those generous folk, familiar with Miss Flaggon's extraordinary athleticism so late in life, were politely astonished to learn of her actual age.

'I'm sorry, Sophie, but I still can't quite believe it,' a kindly local confessed. 'Impossible, when you think about it. So agile. At ninety eight? It's a miracle.'

Others were more prosaic. 'Your grandmother had a bloody good run for her money,' a dealer acquaintance observed, her sigh arced with resentment. 'What a way to expire. Honestly, *Dying Swan* – full make-up, I heard . . . Do you mind if I take a pew?' She folded reverently onto a nearby Ernest Gimson chair, and threw a savage trawl across the room. 'No flowers, Sophie?'

'Mum said she wouldn't want them.'

'Probably best.' The woman wrinkled out a smile and flicked back her untidy fringe. 'Your grandmother took me to my first auction, you know. I was only a kid at the time. Fulham, I think it was. Back in the day when you could pick this stuff up for next to nothing,' she said, stroking the chair's crudely hewn arm, a detail so prized by collectors of that period. 'Loved her little games, did your grandmother.' Her voice eased. 'You have to admit, though, Prune did have a marvellous eye. Like an Exocet missile, it was. And I've always admired her flatware. Did she mention . . . the silver . . . at all, Sophie?'

She hadn't.

'No word on the larger pieces?'

None whatsoever. The worryingly young-for-her-age granddaughter had bagged the entire estate, from apartment down to the cutlery.

All eyes were now on this artless beneficiary. A eulogy, perhaps?

Even through the fog of grief and shocking fortune, Sophie could not unblemish the memory of her granny, or their final conversation. She swayed on the spot, words lumpy in her mouth. 'Granny was . . .'

The kindly local, his thoughts softer on the relative than the deceased, swiftly captured the elusive phrase. 'Your grandmother was a real *character*, darling. In every way.'

'Eccentric,' someone else offered.

If anyone's reputation required the judicious epithet, it was not Prunella's. She'd loathed propriety, commending to the virtuous the riches of glorious damnation. And if the sanctimonious ever came to crow, she'd taken great delight in tarring them with one large offending brush.

Sophie knew all this, aware that an offendee or two may even be present. 'She could be a bit difficult,' she stammered. 'But Granny was nearly a hundred, and I can't believe she's not here.'

A voice wafted from the doorway. 'Almost a centenarian,' it observed. 'So near and yet so far. Ladies and maligned minorities, a toast. Here's to our enchantingly wicked Prunella. We're not convinced you've gone.'

A thin patter of laughter and a chorus of 'to the wicked Prunella' fell like rain. Eyes momentarily considered the dazed granddaughter, and then returned to their empty glasses.

'Well done, love.' The upstairs neighbour appeared, and gave Sophie's arm a gentle pat. 'There certainly won't be one like your grandmother in a hurry,' she assured, waving an unlit cigarette. 'Course, I'm hardly ever here these days. Got a little place in France now. Only found out about Prune last week.' She directed her gaze to the room. 'Christ, all this crap to sort out. Never seen anything like it, Sophie. And I can't believe that bed, love. It's like a bloody sarcophagus.'

Sophie couldn't remember what a sarcophagus was.

'I may consider renting upstairs out now,' the woman advised, her head inclined, capturing a distant memory. 'The estate agents kept her very quiet. I remember my first day here. She was in her garden, half past nine in the morning and stark naked but for the shadow of next door's washing. She was well into her seventies, even then.' A reassuring smile was summoned. 'I'm not saying there was anything wrong with it, love. Just that Prune could not live without an audience, no matter how small.' The smile puckered. 'Would I have bought if I'd known about Prune? Difficult to say,' she answered herself. 'By the way, where did your poor mum disappear to?'

'Got the train back,' Sophie mumbled into her glass.

'And left you all on your own? That's a shame. Still, Scotland is a hell of a long way, and I'll be honest with you, I'm surprised she arranged this spread, considering. Probably terrified the old witch will come back and haunt her. By the feel of this place, I think she already has.'

She rested the cigarette on her bottom lip. 'Just nipping outside for a smoke, love.'

A soft, salty bubble escaped down the granddaughter's cheek.

The art dealer, who had not moved from her seat, stood suddenly. Resolute against tearful distractions, she reached out in supplication. 'For God's sake, do not let the charity shops near any of this. They're absolute crooks,' she said, and pressed a scrap of paper into Sophie's hand. 'My number. I'll come back when you're feeling stronger. Call, if you need to talk,' she mumbled, and slipped away.

More guests squeezed in and out of the apartment, some well acquainted with the dead woman, others shockingly new to the phenomenon that was Prunella Flaggon. Tales of bizarre happenings and unresolved events were squirreled away to be picked over in private exchanges.

Sophie drifted off to the kitchen. The hardly-ever-here neighbour had finished her cigarette and tottered in from the garden, a thin hand fanning the stench of tobacco. 'It's colder in than out. For God's sake, get central heating, love. She might've lived in the bloody nineteenth century, but you don't have to. It's more basic than rural France.'

Sophie wasn't listening and closed the kitchen door behind her. She pulled up a stool and sat staring blankly at the night-filled window – her mixed-up guilty sadness swallowed and unshared.

Eventually the dull drone of conversation faded and

guests crept in to bid farewell. Eyes lingered and weighed their little calculations, distant murmurings of good luck and gasps of genuine amazement at the lateness of the hour. They absolutely had not intended to stay so long.

The few caring types had cleared away the mess – the rest, noting their hostess in morbid contemplation, collected the best unopened bottles and departed, their cynical appraisals blowing like those autumn leaves, and left withering at the gate.

'That's put the cat amongst the pigeons. Her poor mother was completely overlooked. I mean, how would you feel?'

'And Sophie hasn't got a clue. For her age? She's got to be at least thirty. I feel a bit sorry for her, actually.'

'Why? Even in that state the place is worth a bloody fortune. What a waste. And she drinks like a fish.'

'Yes, I noticed that. Depressive, I'd say. She was totally dominated by you know who, don't speak ill of the dead.'

'But we do, the mad, selfish bitch. Anyway, I'll pop in during the week.'

'I think she'll be okay. I'm at the church on Wednesday. I'll look in myself, after our Alpha meeting.'

They wouldn't, of course.

(St. Mortgage's)
The Rising Price of Property in Twickenham

Sophie

When Sophie eventually stirred, it was almost light. Beyond the kitchen window, a thin sun trickled over the magnolia tree, scattering watery beads across the garden fence.

She made a swift overview of her situation. Granny: gone. Funeral: done. Party thing: over. How did she feel today? Funny. Really peculiar.

Her former housemates, two of her colleagues from work, were already finding someone to pay her share of the rent. They were really sorry about her loss and hoped she'd feel better soon, but it was totally amazing about the new place. Yet none of them had visited and Sophie remained in the flat, waiting for it to be finally, legally hers.

Inheritance is a bittersweet thing. The beneficiary can't evince too much pleasure at receiving the sum total of a deceased's providence, but neither should they be so crass as to instantly dispose of it. Sophie showed neither delight nor haste. She was simply overwhelmed. There was so much.

The ground floor maisonette was a short walk from the railway station in one of the many roads once owned by the Church. Over the years, these modest but 'well placed' homes were sold off and the area became increasingly desirable. These days properties changed hands for vast sums, mostly from the pesky

Johnnies-come-lately, slightly less discerning than those creeping in on the likes of Twigmere – ruining everything with righteous jogging and ostentatious parenting. Buyers soon found the flats in St Mortgage's were noisy and pokey, with overlooked gardens too small to swing a Buddhist gong in.

Prunella had found the soaring prices in her humble manor entertaining. She wooed the bourgeoning supply of estate agents, getting them to look around and write valuations, which she'd pin up with other appraisals collected over the decades.

'Sophie,' she'd say, in a lather of mischief, 'I realise this is not your thing, but the vultures have been around again. New talons on the block. Three-quarters of a million, these are now. Even *un-modernised*. Already had two viewings and several more booked in.'

'You shouldn't lead people on.'

'Don't be such heavy weather. One has to rise to the absurd. And you could have an interest here one day, my girl, so don't turn your nose up.'

That was the only clue that Sophie had of her windfall – even then, being the ponderous girl she was, she didn't cotton on. Up to now, the shadowy distractions of property values, investments or even antique dealers had not darkened her path.

She stood and gave a stretch, swaying her arms back and forth in the small kitchen. Someone had left a plate of curled up sandwiches in the pantry. She crammed a couple in her mouth and swallowed the dry bread triangles in one unchewed gulp. Staggering to the living room, she made it to the long settee, dropped onto its sturdy springs and fell asleep.

2014
Hertfordshire

Lydia Wakes from a Dream & A Seductive Sofa

Lydia jolted awake to a respectful rap on the front door and rolled over on the sofa. She sagged on the edge for a few seconds, cradling two large cushions. For some reason this was the front room. Where's that bloody bed? And her toe hurt.

The rapping persisted a little louder. About time a proper bell was fitted. She levered herself upright, flung back the cushions and hobbled to the door.

Shapes were moving behind the stained glass. Two worrying, big men shapes that lilted from side to side. Slowly turning the latch, she found the mattress-turner's little red business card stuck to her wrist and was about to peel it off, when, 'Mrs. Jellow?'

In the narrow and as yet barren front garden, two of the neatest and most exemplary specimens of human deference stood before her and smiled. They were showing her a sheet of paper with her name and address on. 'Mrs. Jellow,' they repeated, 'you are expecting a bed recently purchased from Glee's Bedding of Twigmere?'

Am I? Lydia wanted to say. Are you going to take the one upstairs back? she wanted to ask. But instead, she nodded and slumped giddily against the wall.

While the men withdrew to attend to their delivery, she trudged up the stairs to check the bedroom. It was empty and showed no evidence of being sullied by creatures of the cabbage fields. It was the same fragrant space she believed she'd left less than hour before. Mrs. Jellow either had fallen asleep on that sofa or was still dreaming.

Leaning over the banister, she watched the men, now donning taupe dustcoats, arrive in the hallway. They looked up. 'No need for concern, Mrs. Jellow,' they chorused brightly. 'You can relax, we'll manage it all. But if you wouldn't mind telling us whether it will be a north to south or east to west position?'

Good sweet God. How the hell do I know?

'We do have a compass, Mrs. Jellow, if you are uncertain.'

The sun rises in the east; that much she knew. 'I think it gets the sun in the morning,' she said and darted into the bathroom.

Ear pressed to the door, she listened to the movers' discreet dance: the shuffle, the creaking twist to accommodate the bulk, followed by the patter of quick, close footsteps as they politely negotiated the thin hallway. Even the whoosh of the bed's polythene covering as it slid against the wall sounded apologetic. It would do, she realised. Only in such twilight worlds can activities of this kind be so perfectly executed.

The men had reached the landing, where she imagined them swiftly and adroitly guiding the item into the bedroom. There then ensued a respectful and gratified silence.

Lydia emerged and took a bold look. There it was, or wasn't: stripped naked of its plastic caul, a new age of slumber was born. Gorgeous, it was bloody out of this world. That hand-stitching, the piping, the perfectly puckered edges, certainly worth all of the seven or whatever grand she'd paid. And the divan. No one really cares about a divan yet this, snug beneath its mattress, with its softly curved edges, pristine in crisp blue-and-white ticking was adorable. How did they get that up the stairs without her noticing? Should she tip them? 'I'll find something for you two,' she sang, skipping lumpily down the stairs.

In the front room, the delivery men stationed themselves by the fireplace. Lydia noticed their dustcoats bore a lilac embroidered emblem, which she couldn't quite make out.

'Mrs. Jellow, we've taken the liberty of placing your bed in the north south position,' the older one informed her, 'which is recommended as the most favourable for restorative sleep. As you are continuing with Glee's services, we advise that the mattress be turned within the next three months.'

As Lydia hastily crumpled up a couple of notes from her purse, the younger of the delivery men stepped forward and handed her a clipboard. 'If you could sign here, please, Mrs. Jellow. This is to confirm that you are satisfied with our excellent service.'

'Oh, yeah, sure.' She took the pen, dream over.

The men turned to leave.

'Just a sec.' She held the notes aloft. The clipboard man shook his head and imparted an expression that implied: No gratuities; excellence is our reward, and gently closed the door behind them, soundlessly as a head touching a down pillow.

Alone, Lydia eyed the stairs. 'Fine,' she said. 'Let's see how long this one lasts,' and she climbed to the bedroom.

The mattress was still there, its delicate, rippling pearl-shaped pockets bathed in near religious calm. A headboard, upholstered in Morris & Co print damask, hung over the stillness like an altar. She couldn't remember ordering that headboard, but never mind.

It was a relief to find the walls were not closing in, as in that nightmare, and she moved across to touch the mattress. Soft. She pressed: firm, and pressed harder: politely resistant. She sat on the edge and gave a little jump: pliant but not needy. She bounced again: accommodating yet with self respect. Raising her legs, she swung up and stretched out. The bed received her ample form as if in accord with an anticipated meeting, intuitively adjusting to every motion.

A nervous glance over her feet to a view of the stairs confirmed nothing untoward there. The Welsh blanket lay folded on the chair, as it had been in the last encounter. Outside, beyond the window, the scratchy outline of trees, a few clouds drifting across the sky as the world carried on.

Would the bed's perfection survive? Once more she tried to picture Mr. Gifford Hans. Where was that card? Reluctantly she rose from the bed, her fingers lingering over its sculpted contours.

She went downstairs and realised that she'd forgotten to make a note of the name on that van. Did it matter? Anyway, why should anyone else be treated to that bespoke service? Best keep this one to herself.

She threw a wary eye over the sofa, then, gathering her handbag, tossed on a coat and left the house before dreaming or reality, whichever one it was, could cheat her again.

2014
Twickenham

Sophie

A Slow Dawn

Prunella had dressed the bed as usual that last morning. A wide sash of tasselled brocade constrained the mattress like a giant cummerbund. Fine tapestry cushions were scattered across its vast satin belly, and deep pillows in their white monogrammed shams scudded like clouds across the ornate headboard.

The room was freezing. Every so often, the window rattled and an icy gust leaked into the room.

Sophie looked across to the wardrobe doors pushed ajar by the bulge of clothes. A pair of satin ballet shoes, their long ties like empty arms, reached out in the greedy darkness. She glanced down and considered her own plump, un-balletic feet.

In the weeks following her grandmother's funeral, she hadn't touched a thing. Maybe she imagined Prunella would sweep in and reclaim the accumulation of that eccentric life. For without this burden of riches, she hadn't so much lost a grandmother as been relieved of one.

The Flaggon history was a complicated affair. Sophie, like her mother, had been a late and only child, brought up in what turned out to be a single household, her own father now rarely in contact.

Mum and Prunella had argued since she could

remember, mainly about Sophie's estranged grandpa. After years of rancour, the mum took the grandpa's side, while Prunella commandeered Sophie. Then the grandpa died. Shortly afterwards the mother made a big hysterical scene at the Twickenham apartment, calling Prunella a tyrant and monster. She claimed that her poor sweet father, if in fact he *was* her father, had been treated abominably and that his 'very odd' death (Mum really did wonder about that) and wretched funeral, was so shameful that she'd wanted to kill herself. Or possibly (and the world would surely thank her) Prunella. In the event, she'd moved to Edinburgh, while Sophie stayed behind. Just as well.

That was fifteen years ago.

Tyrant and monster maybe, but Prunella was once unwitting vanguard. All those excoriating judgements on sour, independent females could easily, in part, be applied to her.

Grandpa had been enfeebled, emasculated by his love for the older, flame-haired siren. Not only did Prunella cruelly refuse to marry him, an indulgence akin to madness in those far-off days, she'd insisted their bastard child be registered under the maternal name alone. 'Father' could be around whenever he wished but as far as anything else went, she would manage perfectly well without him.

Surely this was not a conscious and early stand for female politics? Prunella did not follow or empathise with anyone. The dreadful woman simply enjoyed an indecently long life, with a consummate preoccupation with herself. Possibly.

What about the granddaughter? She must have

singled her out for some consideration; after all, there was the inheritance. Yet, like those ill-matched ballet shoes and rails of antique couture, it could hardly be described as fitting.

It is often said that family characteristics skip a generation. If this were true, Sophie needed to get a move on in the wickedness department.

Winter 2014
Twigmere

Third Benjamin
Issues of a Material Nature
&
A Disappearing Grate

A thread of crimson lit the small hill – higgledy roofs embroidered in the setting sun – exquisite, but too perfect to be real.

On this cold Tuesday in mid-December, Twigmere's conservation area retained an element of otherness. Its knot of cottages with their low doors and hanging fish-scale tiles, were enchanting yet, Ben presumed, must be stiflingly small within.

This first visit to the mattress turner's twee address might have been enjoyable, and most certainly interesting, were it not for the error that prompted it. Whose error had yet to be established, but the young proprietor was convinced it was not his own.

Ben had become accustomed to Mr. Hans's appearances at the shop, and his bizarre collection of spectacles had long ceased to amuse him. It was only since taking over the Twigmere business that he'd been actually disturbed by the peculiar ways.

Being of a thorough nature, Ben unearthed old files his father, Joseph, kept, and discovered that Mr. Hans's services were not revived until quite recently.

Further research revealed that great-great-grandpa Benjamin H. Glee created the position of 'Uniquely

Personal Conveniences' for a Mr. G. Hans, esquire on November 22nd 1859. The arcane document bore two faded signatories, witnessed by Benjamin's wife with her mark. Since then, it seemed, Messrs Hans had kept a curiously possessive rein on acquired clients. Each customer's now illegible name, address and even date of birth had been logged and any annotations meticulously recorded below. But why, Ben wondered, would his equally cautious father bother to rekindle such a strange partnership when he was so near to his retirement? One, sadly, he would not live to enjoy.

The ledgers held yet more intrigue. This reference to Gifford Hans had continued unbroken in entries for over one-and-a-half centuries. Having only sons was not so unusual, but to all have the same given name? Then again, he was the third Benjamin in his family.

Anyway, none of this stuff really mattered, it was the present circumstances around the old man that troubled him. For a start, there was the obvious question of how someone as old as Hans could carry out the heavy work on his own. If he was enlisting outside help then this threw up all sorts of problems.

Absorbed in these concerns, he approached the cottages. 'Eleven, fifteen, eighteen,' he counted. Some numbers were missing, but then he saw the ornate brass knocker, with *Hans G. Esquire* engraved above, and rapped. Interesting rope-design, he thought, or was that a snake? The door eased open.

Mr. Hans, wearing a smart grey suit and lemon cravat, regarded him severely through a pair of round, electric-blue spectacles. He emerged from his doorway and seemed to loom and spill out onto the pavement, forcing the young proprietor to take a backward step into some iron railings.

'Good afternoon, Mr. Glee,' he intoned evenly. 'How may I help?'

Ben placed a steadying hand behind him. 'I've a letter, an entry,' he stammered, 'about an address.' Now flattened against the railings, the only barrier between him and the busy road beneath, he felt defensive and indignant. It wasn't his fault if the old fool didn't have a phone of any description and wouldn't answer his letters.

Hans, suddenly alert to his visitor's discomfort, smiled graciously. 'Mr. Glee, won't you come in?' He motioned toward the door. 'Please, we can talk inside.'

Ben composed himself and followed the man into the cottage. The place was indeed tiny. Faded, patchy wallpaper peeled and bubbled in the dank air, dark-stained floorboards were scuffed, the yellow pine flecking the surface like light through a moth-eaten curtain.

Mr. Hans was speaking. 'May I offer you refreshments?'

'No,' Ben said quickly. 'I'm fine. Thank you.'

The old man gestured to a single upholstered chair. 'Please.'

Ben lowered himself on the edge of the seat and rubbed his hands together. The room was arranged in an almost perfect triangle, and very cold. The only possible source of heat was from a cast-iron fireplace stuck right in the corner, and that was dead. A bed, a rickety iron thing, was shoved against a wall, a tapestry rug thrown over the mattress in an attempt to dignify it.

He tried to imagine the Hans family living here, the long line of Giffords spending their respective winters in this miserable, misshapen place. And where would they sleep? He looked around for the stairs. Were there stairs off the hallway? Ben couldn't even remember if they'd entered via a hallway. Glancing up at a clock on the mantelpiece, he saw that was wrong, too – stopped at just after five-to-seven – another useless antique.

Mr. Hans removed his glasses and leaned against the fireplace, resting an elbow on the narrow mantelpiece. 'May we begin?'

Ben peered up, but the light was poor and the old man's face was in shadow.

As if hearing the visitor's thoughts, he moved his hand across and clicked on a lamp; it cast a feeble orange glow. 'Now, Mr. Glee, what is the purpose of your visit?'

'I apologise for disturbing you,' the proprietor began, tersely, 'but I feel, due to your insistence on detail, that we need to look at a few issues, in person.'

'Issues?'

'There've been a couple of minor instances that . . . surprised me.' Ben listened to his words fall away. It would be best to steer conversation toward the gentleman's long service and his health. Look at him, he was ridiculously old. His attention strayed to a bundle of letters next to the hearth – the names and addresses on them looked familiar. He marshalled his thoughts and pressed on. 'I sent you details of a new customer a while back. Since then, she has . . . ' Ben broke off.

Hans was slowly crossing the room. He reached the bed and creaked down with a doleful sigh.

Ben felt a surge of pity. The poor soul lives like a pauper. He thought of his own frail mother, and how he'd feel if she lived alone like this, her mind failing. 'I won't keep you long, Mr. Hans. We're doing very well, with several new clients all eager to take advantage of erm, your exclusive and unique service.' He smiled, suddenly conscious of the preposterous statement. 'You will remember a new customer by the name of Jellow. She purchased a low to mid-range mattress almost a year back, but she has since . . .'

Mr. Gifford Hans's features suddenly blossomed and he beamed at his guest. 'I am fully cognisant of the client's peripatetic temperament. Is this where you believe the error lies?'

'Cognisant? Peripatetic?' Ben repeated to himself. Why on earth would the old chap say something like that? 'Well, Mr. Hans, I can't . . . I did write regarding her new address, but I see that you've reverted to the old one.'

The other man still smiled broadly, his eyes a summer blue. 'I have made a note of the address. All of the addresses are noted and there have been many.' He bent forward slightly to emphasise the point. 'Mr. Glee, no error has been made. Hertfordshire. The town in question is a most pleasing settlement of some antiquity, if the traveller enjoys a long, linear high road.'

The proprietor was baffled. 'I couldn't say, Mr. Hans, but why have you put the old address back in the diary? This changing back and forth is very confusing.' Ben shifted uncomfortably in his seat. 'In fact, that is not the only problem. You were due to attend to another customer on Christmas Eve. The lady, a well established client, is no longer with us.'

The lamp on the mantelpiece flickered and the old man's mood became suddenly overcast. 'I am apprised of the conditions to which you refer: the most recent address and my pending appointment.'

'But you no longer have an appointment. There is *no customer* . . . We were informed – ' Here, Ben struggled to remember when and how he knew. 'I did write to you about this, but I find that you've crossed out an appointment for a new customer and kept hers, the, er, deceased's, in the book. Our prospective, *living* client who's been patiently waiting will be very disappointed.'

That was harsh, Ben thought. He considered the gaunt figure before him. It couldn't wait. It was time to confront the inevitable. 'I wanted to thank you for . . .' he began. 'I wanted to . . .' he coughed and started again. 'I . . ' His words, rather than being delivered in his usual measured monotone, issued in jerky squeaks, like strangled cries. He could not find his voice, or if it was there, the sound was inaudible to him. Trying again, his words, the questions desperate for expression began to unravel, fade and finally vanish from his mind as though they had never been formed.

He bolted upright in his chair, Mr. Hans's low humming the only sound drifting to his ears. He wasn't certain of the tune, but by some preternatural means understood that tangled in its melody was a chiding – a warning, most certainly that, and almost a threat.

At last, his throat opened and he breathed once

more. 'I'm glad we've managed to sort that out, Mr. Hans. The lady was a loyal client for many years. I'm gratified this appointment will be kept and trust many more will continue far into the future. Good evening and a happy Christmas.'

Mr. Gifford Hans moved wordlessly to the door and drew it back for the young proprietor and unwitting bearer of strange tradition to leave.

Outside in the sweetly biting air, Ben was greeted by a silhouette of trees, their tall outline silvered by a drawing frost. He felt strangely unburdened and at peace. What a man Mr. Hans was. It was a privilege to know such a remarkable person. If you thought about it, which he probably never did in quite the same way again.

Within the leaden geometry of that ascetic dwelling, Gifford Hans was crouched over the fireplace, setting light to sheaves of paper. He bowed nearer the growing flames, his hands clasped to his face in an attitude of either penance or deep mourning. Reaching up, he felt blindly for the wooden clock, shook it and flicked open the glass face. Staggering away, he placed a trembling finger on the minute hand, gingerly moving it forward it until it described fifteen minutes past eight o'clock. Shaking his head in frustration, he returned again to the small hand and delicately nudged it back one minute more. He snapped the glass shut, stretched up and returned the clock to its iron shelf.

For one fleeting moment the fire exploded into fanning flames, appearing to consume the wretched man and all that was in the room.

Winter 2014

Almost a Centenarian, God Disposes
&
Sophie Starts to Dig

Prunella had given no instructions as regards her remains. Why bother? Life was dust, she was dust, and eternity probably a vacuum cleaner. If that were the case, there was one proviso: just make sure you use a new bag. I do not wish to be blended with some decrepitude on a mobility scooter.

'Granny, you'll live for ever.'

'That's why I mentioned it.'

Her antique shell abandoned, Miss Flaggon's remains were contained in a modest receptacle and stored on a shelf in a nearby funeral parlour.

Several weeks on, Sophie awoke one mid-morning to a thud of reckoning. Bad Granny was still waiting to be collected and, despite the deceased's laissez-faire attitude toward her disposal, it could not be ignored forever.

Cloaking on a bedspread, Sophie padded barefoot to the chaotic kitchen. After washing down her porridge with a cupful of wine, she slung the dish into the sink and wandered to the settee, empty cup in hand. Then it was back for a refill.

Her first call was to the funeral directors, the next to someone in the 'resting place' department – both conversations carried out in varying states of befuddlement. Satisfied that everything was arranged,

Sophie pottered about the flat, aimlessly moving things. Finding a tersely worded letter from work, she tore it up and chucked it with the others.

When she arrived at the funeral directors the following day, a smiling employee presented her with a green package.

She received it as one would a gift, a nicely boxed cake from an expensive confectioner. Seeing Prunella's name flourished on the side, she said, 'This is her? Okay. I'm glad she's not mixed up. My grandmother so did not want to be mixed up.'

The employee completely understood about that, assuring her the utmost care was taken in such matters.

Once outside, Sophie eased her charge into a plastic carrier bag. Now for the next ordeal.

Her procrastinations regarding the ashes were probably due to lack of scattering options. What element could absorb the remnants of an unconscionable rogue? The river risked blowing them back in her face, the countryside would have no meaning, and a final home in the bequeathed residence was out of the question. Failing all else, there was one place that must surely take a fallen soul. Ironic, really, knowing Prunella's thoughts on the subject.

She arrived at the church just as the charismatic vicar was closing a meeting. Choosing a pew, she crinkled the bag on an embroidered cushion and waited.

The vicar breezed up. He seemed surprised. 'Good morning and welcome to our family.' Leaning over the pew, fingers suitably interlocked, he said, 'Are you here for our introduction?'

Sophie shook her head. 'The other end. I rang you yesterday, about my granny.'

The vicar's smooth face affected a puzzled expression. He loosened his hands. 'And you are?'

'Sophie. Her granddaughter.'

'Remind me, had a busy week.'

'You said you'd take my granny. She didn't actually attend, but she lived here for ages.'

'Did I say that? That I'd take your granny?'

'She was ninety-eight when she passed.' Sophie patted the carrier bag. 'In here.'

'Right. Almost a centenarian.' The vicar delicately turned his vestment sleeve and then checked his watch. 'Let's go outside, Sophie.'

On the porch, they both stood contemplating an unwelcome patch of freezing land.

The vicar said, 'We don't really do ashes, Sophie. I assume they are – '

'This bit is consecrated, though, isn't it?'

'What I'm trying to say, is that this is a garden and not a depository.'

'I thought I could plant something with her, an azalea thing, or whatever. It would still be a garden.'

'But you'd need to care for your azalea 'thing', and we have our own gardeners. It would get confusing. And what happens if it dies?'

Sophie felt a thrill of righteous affirmation, a Prunella litany buzzing at her ear: what a surprise! Resurrection? In a church? You won't find that kind of thing in there, my girl. It's all "Daddy loves me" and sibling rivalry in that circus.'

She looked down at the plastic handles cutting into her wrist, and felt more foolish than usual. 'Okay. Thanks.'

'God bless, Sophie. I hope you find a suitable home for your granny.' He twisted away to acknowledge a group of ripe young mums silently rejoicing 'saved' beneath a thunderous sky. 'Come back soon,' he called to her.

Sophie skewered him in her mind. 'Sod off,' she said, which was unlike her.

1949
Twigmere

Joseph
&
Others Previously Met

The war missed Twigmere and continued twenty six miles south to jettison its bombs on Portsmouth, then moving a little west, dropped the rest on Southampton. The Germans had no truck with a rural backwater, even if it did have an excellent railway.

Twigmere mourned its fallen overseas, their names, along with those from the first war, duly engraved on the roll of honour. The young evacuees from London and the other large conurbations were long since returned to their city homes. The war was over, business was picking up and beds were being sold.

Benjamin Glee hadn't touched the war, first or second. Prestige in all its myriad forms was the only thing he fought for.

At a majestic six foot two and with a head of thick, black hair, the proprietor showed no visible signs of having recently passed his seventieth year. Since taking over the business from his father, he'd done very well for himself and the shop was a veritable cornucopia of the highest quality furniture for the bedroom, and beyond.

'Pop' Jacob, on the other hand, was not blessed with the good fortune of his son, or the famed longevity of his own father. He caught a chill after a stormy crossing to the Isle of Wight and, after a brief illness, expired peacefully at the tender age of fifty seven. His dear wife and childhood sweetheart, Minnie, died of grief six months later.

Benjamin himself became a widower at thirty nine and with no issue from that union, married again. In 1942, his second wife also lost her foothold on life's perilous ledge, when she plummeted from a faulty funfair contraption at Margate sands. Miraculously, their infant son, Joseph was spared – propelled from his mother's arms into a basket of rotting vegetables on a nearby stall. At the time, Mr. Glee was attending to war supplies in Ramsgate and did not witness the tragic accident. Now he brought up his young son with the help of various admiring females.

On this particular afternoon, he entertained the least adoring female he knew. It was late September and the weather, taking a turn for the glorious, offered the proprietor some relief from the exotic and not entirely welcome company.

To give the lady his undivided attention, he'd closed for the afternoon. She would have expected nothing less. They stood together in the autumnal sun, the music low on a brand-new wireless set. Occasionally Benjamin would glance over his shoulder to peer out at the street, as if expecting someone.

Mr. Glee had known his visitor since she was a babe in the arms of her charming mother. Now, at twenty nine, (or thirty, no one was quite sure), she was still captivating. The abundant hair had lost none of its flaming red, nor the skin its milky hue; grey-blue eyes still glistened with mischief and the nature remained startlingly determined: Prunella Flaggon was the epitome of blooming health and wilfulness. And to add a touch of poignancy, she was an orphan.

Perched on a magnificent display bed, an antelope-skin coat hooding her petite form, she gestured toward the bed's carved headboard. 'Is this really *the* best, Mr. Glee?'

The shopkeeper gave a throaty laugh. 'After it be stripped down, perhaps this particular model ain't quite *the* best,' he admitted, suspicion in his narrowing eyes. 'But the company does make beds for royalty under warrant, far back, as well you know. And given the quality, for the price, it is perfect and offers great durability.'

'And what price your durability, Mr. Glee? I've often wondered.'

He waved a finger in mock annoyance, his tone uncertain. 'Now, now. You mustn't play games with me, young Prunella. We don't discuss them things.'

She ran a dainty hand across the dense mattress. 'It does look so cumbersome. How is it to be aired?'

Before he could answer, his guest fell back, fainting on the bed. With both red hair and her vast coat billowing around her, it appeared, in that upside-down world, like a poppy field landing on a parachute.

At first, the canny proprietor dismissed this as Flaggon theatrics, but on noting her extreme pallor, rushed to a door beneath the mezzanine. 'Joseph!' he roared. 'Bring water!'

Footsteps thundered across the building, and a stubby lad of about eight appeared at the foot of the stairs.

'She's fainted, son. Water, salts. Hurry.'

By the time the boy returned with a cup, the

swooning woman had recovered. She raised herself, smiling weakly. 'Thank you, kind Joseph.'

Mr. Glee set the water down. 'You fainted, my little hen. Are you not feeding yourself?'

Prunella draped a hand across her brow and gave a tragic sigh. 'I fear there will soon be someone else to feed,' she said, and prostrated herself on the bed once more. 'What with nausea, loss of gravity and thinning of the bones, they say it's terribly bad for dancers,' she murmured, one gimlet eye gauging his reaction.

Scarlet comprehension, thunderous clouds and white fury awakened in gradual succession across the proprietor's heavy features. He strode to the wireless and snapped the music off.

Prunella studied him with impish curiosity. 'Benjamin, you do look cross.'

He slotted his thumbs in his waistcoat pockets, mouth slack with ostentatious disappointment. 'Now you behave, young madam. If I understands you right, this ain't the time to talk of prancing. You're acting like it's happening to someone else.'

'In a way it is. And I'll manage. I always do.' She uncurled, stretching languorously on the coverlet, her fingertips barely reaching the edges of the mattress. 'Sadly, however, I am now in need of a discreet abode.'

'Just *I* is it? No mention of the other poor beggar involved? I expect he's already had his marching orders now the deed is done.'

She wriggled to the edge of the bed and dangled her feet. 'Forget him. An innocent expedient. He can think as he wishes.'

'You've no heart, and him worshipping the ground

you walk, I'll wager.'

'And you such an old-fashioned, honourable creature are offended on his behalf? I think not, Mr. Glee. Accommodation is the most pressing concern. All else will follow.'

He removed his fob watch, and fingered its gold case.

'Don't sulk, Benjamin. Probity does not become either of us. We must be practical.' She kicked her legs, dainty shoes tipping from her heels. 'You know I've always relied on you.'

He crossed to the window and stared out in silence, eyes darting fearfully along the street. 'And I'm to blame for letting you. What with the little games you've played over the years.'

'As have you,' she reminded him. 'We're equal in that.'

The shopkeeper swung around, his eyes black. 'You got the cheek of the devil. Some of us has responsibilities. This ain't a lark, woman.' He returned to his vigil, eyes now lost in the quiet street. On the hotel opposite, shadows were already slinking across its ivy-clad walls. Within the shop, time breathed silently, air stilled.

'There's one possibility, in Middlesex,' he said, suddenly. 'Part of a lot I acquired by mischance. I only seen it once. Ain't much, but it be vacant. Better used and gain value, than disposed of at a loss.'

Prunella clapped her hands in delight. 'Bravo, dear Benjamin. I have that small allowance to live on. The result of a careless nod on a Middlesex plot will surely be a marvellous investment.'

'Ain't me that's careless. And there ain't no such

thing as accidents.' Returning the watch to his waistcoat, he surveyed her with the sufferance of a guardian toward a recalcitrant charge. 'But it never were a game and I hope it ain't a boy.'

'Accident or design, don't it skip a generation, Mr. Glee?' she laughed, affecting his coarse burr. 'We can't be too serious, though, can we? Far too late for that,' She toppled like a floppy doll into his arms.

Young Joseph, who'd silently witnessed the puzzling scene unfold, crept noiselessly back to the door and tiptoed upstairs to his bedroom.

He climbed on his bed and pushed open a small casement window. Leaning on the windowsill, the boy had a good view of the High Street. There he was again.

An old man, smartly dressed in a cream linen suit and wearing a distinctive pair of tortoiseshell *pince-nez,* came into view. He was walking in the direction of the shop, tapping his stick on the shadowy pavement as he went. As the man drew near, he glanced up and, noticing the boy, nodded.

Even from where he knelt, Joseph could see the bright blue eyes flash. He shivered, and pulled the curtain to, leaving just a crack. Concealed at his vantage point behind the half-closed curtain, he saw the man look up again, lightly touch his hat before turning and heading toward the Town Hall.

The band music from the shop wireless drifted upstairs. Joseph jumped on his bed and pulled a comic from beneath his pillow. Scrabbling among the pages, he slid out a loose sheet of paper and, taking a pencil from his pocket, slowly wrote down what he had seen.

2014
Twickenham

The Worm's Turn & a Crowded Study

Sophie unpeeled the box's packaging and plucked out the metal urn, setting it down at the back of the desk. Next to everything else it looked very modern.

Above, the window frame rattled – she stood and leaned on the damp sash, securing its catch as best she could, and returned to her seat at the desk.

On the faded red leather, fingers of winter sun scratched out a dusty history; a few postcards with old-fashioned writing lay criss-crossed, their edges creased. An open wallet, leaking a bundle of folded notes, was propped on a large diary, itself caught in a loop of jewellery. She hesitated, lifted the wallet, placing it carefully aside, and shook the journal free.

She clambered up onto the bed and rolled onto her stomach, propping the diary on the pillow. An embossed silver 195 swirled on the black cover, a worn patch where the last digit was missing or had been ripped away. Sophie opened the diary and flicked through stiff, blank pages until she came to March 7[th.] A small black and white photograph of a very young Prunella was stapled to the top corner. Strange, she thought, that was her own birthday, except she wasn't even born then. There was nothing else until December, and a few numbers scrawled on the last day. Apart from those two entries, the diary was unused.

She returned to the photograph of Granny's unsmiling face – very different from that usual haughty sneer. This must have been taken when she was about her own age. There was something familiar in the eyes, a kind of intentness – a wilfulness that had travelled undiminished through the decades. The stare Sophie now saw had threatened immortality. That was one thing Granny got wrong.

With these thoughts, the extent of her own life appeared to lengthen, as if she were now bound to continue on her behalf. A sunless road, a prolonged journey to be endured, with few companions to help her face the stretch. *'The unborn will not forgive you,'* Granny had said that final night. *'Children will find you out.'*

Over on the desk, Prunella sat amongst the clutter – slight and incongruous, but still living in her own dust.

Sophie shoved the diary aside and squashed her face in the covers. How did she feel now? Nothing, a big hole of nothing. Her body fell suddenly quiet, an unheard whisper among the satin waves. Behind the tears, bright new dreams clamoured, eyelids drowning in the filling light.

1859
Twigmere

Benjamin Horace Glee
A Confession & Fair Exchange is no Robbery

It was mid-October, and the evening sky blushed in a setting sun. Benjamin Glee, a tall, handsome, if brutish figure stood outside his shop, his sleeves rolled up to the elbow and his arms folded. It had been another quiet day.

He nodded to a gentleman sauntering past. The man had been back and forth, casting furtive glances at the window some three or four times that day, but never showing any inclination to enter the premises.

Benjamin nudged at the clay pipe clenched between his teeth. 'Good evening, sir. Was you looking for something in particular?'

The gentleman, of indeterminate age but well into his dotage, tipped his top hat and smiled. 'Are you Mr. Glee?'

'That I am.'

'You have been in this line of business long?'

The old man was well-spoken and well-attired. Benjamin had been owner of the shop for nearly a year, and not set eyes on him before. Clearly he was a stranger, a visitor to Twigmere.

'Not what you'd call long in this one. Business ain't bad, and will do better when the trains come. If them on the railway company ever stops the arguments.'

The stranger came closer and squinted through a pair

of large, round gold-rimmed spectacles. 'Arguments, railways. Yes, quite so. Good. Excellent. You display fine furnishings.'

'And I'll be happy to show you more. We open tomorrow from eight o'clock; every day opening bar Sunday and half day Wednesdays.'

'But no beds.'

'Begging your pardon?' Benjamin frowned, suddenly suspicious. He did not have beds. He could, the shop was big enough, but now he most definitely did not have or want them. 'We cater mostly for the dining and drawing room. Our high-class customers are from Guildford and beyond. We supply to the larger household, but they don't ask for beds.'

The gentleman seemed amused by this oversight, looking all superior about it, thought Benjamin, as if the fellow knew of something, had a trick, and him, a man starting off in this business, had missed it. He felt a tingle of pride heat his face. 'We do quite well. Beds take up too much space, what with headboards and frames. Not to mention the trouble they can give. Our patrons are certain of what to buy at Glee's.'

'Of course,' the stranger acknowledged, lightly, 'you know your clientele best,' and turned, curiously nimble, on his heel.

At fifteen minutes to eight the following morning, Benjamin came downstairs to open the shutters. He was surprised to discover the old man pressed at the window, peering through, a pair of tortoiseshell half-spectacles balanced on his nose.

'Good morning, sir. I am about to pull the awning. We ain't quite ready.'

The visitor withdrew and gazed back at the empty

street, its houses splashed with the white morning sun.

Benjamin had a queer feeling about the old fox's poking around. A rival outlet most likely. He'd heard some in Portsmouth sent agents to sniff about.

Awning extended and church bell sounding the hour, Benjamin gestured to the door. He followed the man into the shop, where chests, wardrobes, carver chairs and oriental rugs were set out across the floor, and stood by a desk.

The old man seemed to scope the display in a wide arc as if taking an inventory. He removed his half-spectacles and lowered cautiously onto a chaise longue, stroking its figured velvet. 'Exceedingly comfortable. You are most fortunate to have such substantial premises. And living quarters above?'

'Five rooms we got,' Benjamin said sharply. 'Why do you make it your concern?'

'I have a proposition, sir.'

At last, the rogue comes clean, breathed Benjamin to himself, and pulled out a new pipe from his waistcoat.

'Perhaps, Mr. Glee, if I could take a little of your time. In private?'

The shopkeeper held the old man in his gaze, thoughts busy. Did this stranger expect him to shut the shop? And it were Friday. Business tended to be brisker on a Friday. 'I don't think it suits me at present,' he said, and glanced at the clock. It was already ten. That was queer, and the street still deserted. Perhaps he could spare a few minutes. He moved to the door, flipped the sign to 'closed' and pulled down the blind. Returning to where the man rested, he drew up a chair, and sat viewing him with a wary eye. 'What's your business, sir? There ain't nothing for sale here but what you see right before you,' he warned, a pinch of tobacco in his fingers.

'Yes,' the visitor returned, evenly. 'I believe this is where the problem lies.'

'Well, I don't offer no sale or return arrangements, if that's what you're after. It clogs the place up, and there's always trouble to follow.'

The gentleman chuckled pleasantly. 'Indeed. No. It is what I do not see that brings me here. Beds.'

'Beds?' Benjamin felt his skin prickle again, and colour rush to his cheeks. Didn't you already hear my views?' he said, angrily. 'It'd change my custom.'

'From a trickle to a gush, I would wager,' said the man with a curious smile. 'From famine to plenty.'

The shopkeeper abandoned his pipe, and pushed nearer, pointing a warning finger. 'What company you been having words with?' he snarled. 'Trickles and famine?' He slammed a hand on his chair. 'I don't deal with travellers, no matter how fancy they be.'

'How is your wife?' the visitor asked suddenly. 'Yet another burden to bear.'

Benjamin's sense of unease deepened. Why would a stranger mention that? He thought of the letter tucked away in a drawer, the one his young wife would find when it was all over. Have the law come for him at last, in the form of this crank? He stared into the man's bright blue eyes. They weren't the eyes of an official, but there was something familiar in their glint. 'I didn't take a name, mister.'

'I carry a letter,' the man said. 'Rest assured, not of the vexatious kind. My missive is one of high recommendation. If you would care to take this, and show it to your … family.' He proffered an envelope, the shopkeeper's name written in a fine hand.

Without lifting his gaze from the visitor, Benjamin impatiently gestured the letter away. 'And why come to me with recommendations?'

'Quite simply, I offer a unique convenience. Its provision enables me to travel the land and make a modest living whilst doing so. I look around your premises and see infinite possibilities. Yet those possibilities are drained away by the limits of your expectations and … should we say, history?'

Once more Benjamin glanced at the clock and was horrified to see that it was twenty minutes past three. He must be in a stupor. The man had sent him to sleep with all his talk, while upstairs, his poor, neglected wife was still recovering in her bed.

The visitor seemed to pick these concerns from his mind. 'I'm sorry to hear of you and your young wife's sad news. Such disappointment, when all else fails.'

The shopkeeper's thoughts began to wander without direction, one thought an echo of the last. He slumped back into his seat, abandoning all vestiges of reason. 'Is this madness punishment for what I done? That deed will haunt me until I'm dead.' The words were uttered before he could stop them.

'And what deed is that?' the visitor enquired.

Benjamin glanced up, his tongue dry with fear, but still the words tumbled. 'In Hindhead it were. An accident, I swear. My temper does it.'

He slumped forward, his large shoulders sagging with relief at last to give up that burden. 'At the inn there. This fella I never seen before started on me, swearing and cursing. On and on goading, wanting to fight. All them navvies half-cut, jeering and calling him on. I scarpered quick as I could and hid outside. My temper were up and I was of a mind to wait and have him.' He paused and snatched a sly glance at his solitary audience.

'Pray, continue,' the old man prompted gently.

The shopkeeper once more bowed his head. 'There was this iron rail broke in the road. I took it for my own defence. I heard the beggar come out still cussing, but the coward were alone this time. So I followed him down the hill till I come close. He turned. I thought he were . . .' Benjamin held his face. 'It weren't meant to, but it's still done.'

The visitor reclined his arm on the chaise longue, features impassive. 'This victim, a querulous business acquaintance, dead instantly, I presume.'

Alert to the trickery, Benjamin jumped to his feet, eyes wild. 'What are you?' he cried. 'If you know of it all, why ask? He were robbing me blind for years. Taking the bread from my family's mouth. Is this what you come for? Say it then!'

The old man remained without expression. 'Be seated, Mr. Glee.'

He obediently fell to his chair.

'Were there witnesses to this deed?'

Benjamin shook his head. 'Only Him, The Almighty seen me in the pitch black. I pelted down that hill. No mortal eye could have seen me or what I done.'

'Did anyone note your departure from the inn at Hindhead?'

'Don't reckon nobody . . .' His voice lowered to a miserable grunt. 'Except them railway navvies.'

'And being billeted nearby, they, of course were blamed.' The old man raised a knowing brow.

'Arguments, broken rails, the London and South Western Railways. Most providential.'

'I still live with it, sir! Murderer. The deed is doubled now. Though no one knows, its curse sticks to me. My own father not long died, my mother fled, the business ruined. Now my poor wife lost our first and can't have no more. She will watch me hang. I'm a dead man now.'

'Mr. Glee, you are just born,' the visitor assured, calmly. 'Damned by one foolish and impetuous miscalculation upon a scoundrel who would take what was rightfully yours? No.' He paused, as if to clarify a certain point. 'It *is* just the one?'

Benjamin drew a sleeve cuff across his face and nodded.

The old man continued. 'It is my belief that you are a man fully repented. Your conscience is torture enough to fashion the wretch I see before me. And there are many paths to redemption.' The visitor's smile was so radiant, his fine features, lit like the sun, banished the shadows from that sombre room. 'I wish to bestow upon you and your grieving wife a precious benefaction: the gift of hope. Call it salvation. It will, as is to be expected, involve a small commitment on your part.'

Although barely understanding him or the humming that filled his ears, Benjamin listened to all the stranger had to say. The old man talked seriously and affectingly of a wretched and abandoned infant soon to be cast into an asylum. He spoke inspiringly of a unique prospect, a new life blessed with beneficence, of wealth increased, well-being and longevity. Finally, he modestly declared his own selfless role in all this.

Such was his gratitude for this kindness that Benjamin Glee agreed to all of the stranger's fantastical proposals, without once considering the aged gentleman's suitability in regard to the position. Beds would do very well, the floor space was ample, they would all do exceedingly well at the newly formed *Glee & Sons. Purveyors of Fine Beds and Furnishings.* And the gift of hope – how could he, owing so much, refuse such charity?

'I am most relieved. It will be a legacy for generations,' the old man concluded. 'And we will keep our account entirely separate, so it will appear as all your doing, Mr. Glee.'

As the visitor prepared to leave, he handed the letter of recommendation to the shopkeeper, who received it now with humility.

Trembling, Benjamin pulled up the blind and opened the door to see the sky now filled with stars. What's happened to the day, Mr …?'

'I will send an agent in due course. You may reach me at the address he will provide,' the gentleman said. Settling his hat firmly on his head, he strolled from the shop and was folded into the night.

Benjamin Glee stood in the doorway for a few moments, letter in his hand. He took it beneath the dim glow of a street lamp and was surprised to discover how fine the stationery was. Turning it over, he was even more astounded to find the seal bore a small distinctive crest. His heart jolted as if struck by lightning. How could he describe the mysterious encounter with a person of such stature, who carries a testimonial from the highest authority in the land?

He couldn't.

Christmas 2014
Hertfordshire

Lydia's Turn & a Glittering Past

Rugged up in faux beaver skin coat, a hat protecting her dyed blonde curls, Mrs. Jellow trudged home with her purchases: local produce from the Christmas farmers' market, and proper groceries from a well-respected store. That's all there was on offer in this place.

Lydia lived for the frenetic pulse of city life, buoyed by the perpetual motion of that covetous mass – dazzling, exclusive shops, the view from vast glass palaces, where free heat and lighting lent a sense of majesty over all she surveyed.

The retail in this town was pathetic. Stunted. And the decorations were feeble. Let's face it, Hertfordshire would always be provincial, no matter how hard it tried.

She would have popped up to Oxford Street to see their lights, except it was *the* appointment this evening. Daft time to pick, *ten* to seven. Why not seven? Half-six? Glee's had sent a card reminding her, a sneaky little '*cancellation fees apply*' tucked at the bottom. The cheeky buggers. And it was just the wrong time of year to stay in for domestics. These people obviously didn't have a life, and assumed no one else did, either.

She'd absolutely no complaints about the bed, and that unasked for headboard watched over her like a guardian angel. Yet during those long months her besotted determination to employ a mattress turner had run its infatuation. Did she really want to hand over seventy quid to a jumped-up carpet beater? And you can't just chuck them out this time of year without a mince pie, followed by a sherry or four. Besides, no one had shaken a mattress belonging to Lydia for a long while and she didn't know how she felt about the interference.

At home, shopping decanted, wine poured and substantial body languishing on the sofa, Mrs. Jellow became sanguine. 'Oh well, I'll cope.' She glanced down at the plump cushions. 'As long as I don't bloody fall asleep.' She checked her watch: just gone six.

Was the bed stripped? Setting down her glass, she tramped upstairs. It was, but the bedroom light radiated a soft, seductive pink. 'That's no good,' she muttered, and switched it off. 'I'll have to change the bulb to interrogation mode.' Satisfied the room was 'wrong idea' proof, she gave that painted mouth a wipe, smoothed down her ringleted mane, and returned to the front room.

At forty minutes past six, she flip-flopped to the kitchen-diner, opened the massive fridge and stuck her head inside.

The first rattle of the knocker went unheard. It was on a third, long and indignant thud that she was finally jolted from her foraging. 'Oh, Christ.' She thundered to the door, and flung it open on to the freezing night. 'Sorry, sorry, didn't hear you. A bell is on order.'

The mattress turner, for it must be him, was barely discernible against the blackness of the street.

'Hellooo,' she cooed. 'Are you there? Is that Mr. Hans?' This was embarrassing.

'Madam. Mrs. Lydia Jellow?'

'That's me.' Lydia took a backward step. 'Oh. Are you . . .? No, you can't be.' She absorbed the vision of the macabre silhouette before her, swiftly assessing its portent, a bloody undertaker, and clutched at her throat. My God, I'm dead already. An image of her prone body on that coma-inducing sofa sprang into her fertile mind: death by upholstery. It was bound to happen.

Meanwhile, the sepulchral vision thus far remained on the threshold. 'I am Mr. Gifford Hans,' it uttered, and proffered a card pincered by two gloved fingers. 'You have a mattress that requires lifting.' And without asking if he could, the man stepped into the expensively decorated hall.

Mrs. Jellow monitored the De Morgan printed walls. 'Oh, do come in, please,' she muttered icily, wanting to add, 'Just to let you know, I have dreams that are so real I get confused. So, if I ignore you and go and lie down and you are real, then that's why – so, sorry in advance. Oh, and mind that wallpaper, it cost a fortune.' Instead, she demurred, 'Can I get you something to eat? You look very old. I mean, cold.'

Mr. Hans beamed. His skin, almost translucent with age, creped in iridescent folds around a generous mouth. He removed his hat and secured it on a hall peg, carefully hooking his silver-topped walking stick on the same.

Something about that walking stick flashed into Lydia's mind. And then she saw his glasses. Oh, my God. 'Where did you get those? They're wild!' she shrieked, pointing at the ruby-studded, silver-filigree-framed spectacles slotted on the old man's nose. 'Very Christmassy. Are those real stones, dear?'

He bowed graciously. 'You are most kind. When it comes to selecting a day's eyewear, I find colour very important. These are Wednesday's spectacles. You do know about Wednesdays?'

She didn't. 'Now, Mr. Hans,' she interrupted briskly, determined to find out what this joke was about. 'So, let's get this straight. Glee's have sent you to turn my mattress, yes?'

'This is certainly the case. If you consult my card you will see that I offer a unique service.'

'Yes, but you are at least a hundred and thirty, Mr. Hans. Even I couldn't budge that thing upstairs, and I'm forty-one.'

'Fifty, madam.'

'Sorry?'

'You celebrated your fiftieth birthday on August the thirteenth this year, madam. You need not be discreet with me.'

Lydia felt her veins turn to ice. This joke was becoming a freak. Where would he get that information? Not her bank card. The electoral register? The ancestry lot? Some companies stop at nothing to get a financial profile.

Mr. Hans moved inexorably towards the stairs.

'Would you like a hot drink, or something?' Lydia warbled.

Perhaps, she reassured herself, this loony was here to check all was well, and those nice, normal men in their taupe coats would come back and do the job. 'I don't think you need to go up there, dear.'

But the man already had one brogued foot on the stairs. Those are good, she thought, distracted by the shoes. Handmade, could be Church's, if they still exist. Even so, the vision of a bespoke corpse spread-eagled over the undulating waves of her mattress was more than she could bear so near to Christmas.

'Come on,' she said, stalking to the kitchen. 'I'm going to make coffee. You're not lifting anything. I'll ring Glee's tomorrow and ask what they're playing at.' She was aware of the old man behind her, like a cold shadow filling the room. Something felt wrong. Pressing down the kettle switch, she thought, I'll make tea instead. That coffee alone would kill him. 'Milk and sugar?' she asked, reaching for the cupboard. 'Oh, and I left the money on the little shelf in the hallway.' She dropped a teabag into a cup and poured the boiled water. 'Although, technically . . .'

'Thank you, Mrs. Jellow,' he interrupted quickly. 'I have indeed collected the fee. A mere gesture, of course. It is most important that we acknowledge a service, or else that service may be perceived as of little value and, in turn, the efficacy reduced in worth.'

Lydia wasn't listening. She deposited the teabag in the bin and carried the cup over to the table. The man didn't move, but thankfully the glasses had gone. 'Sorry you've had a wasted journey, Mr. Hans.'

'A journey is never wasted. There is always something to discover.' Drawing from the pocket of his long coat, he produced three gold wedding bands dangling from a scarlet thread.

Lydia was transfixed.

'I found these beneath your mattress. Please accept my deepest and sincerest apologies, madam.' He coughed into a politely clenched fist. 'Most unusual. Our men are very well trained, but it only takes a moment's distraction to overlook these things, and if ignored much vexation can be anticipated in the years ahead.' Crossing to the table, he gently placed the rings on the varnished pine surface.

'Eh? 'Lydia leaned across and rolled one of the rings over. Instantly recognising the inscription, she recoiled. 'But these are . . . where the hell?'

'The mattress is thoroughly turned, Mrs. Jellow. You will feel the difference, most certainly.'

She issued a broken laugh. Was she afraid? 'Don't give me that. What do you take me for?' she snorted, backing towards the kitchen drawer. 'Are you telling me that in the nanosecond my back was turned, you've been upstairs and lifted a mattress? Forget beds, Speedy Gonzales, you belong in a bloody circus.'

'You misunderstand me, madam. I am returning these items to you. When I adjusted the mattress, as you employed me to do, these were found beneath.'

This was like that sofa nightmare all over again, she thought, and wasn't having any of it. 'Don't give me that. Predators, that's what you lot are. Someone's got a bit of money, because they've been careful, so you come up with the exclusive this and the cashmere that, and then it's the after-sales scam. This time, some cock and bull story about giving a mattress an MOT every three months.' She drew down a gulp of air, but her confidence was failing. 'How could you do this to a poor lonely widow? At Christmas,' she whimpered.

The mattress turner placidly moved a hand over his breast pocket. 'I must attend again in the spring. If I could suggest March the twenty second? Shall I book now?'

Lydia groped for the chair, but it wobbled from her grasp. 'Have you been listening to me?' She eyed the rings. The one with the inscription seemed to wink menacingly up at her. That was from at least four properties ago.

Mr. Hans retreated to the hallway, where he silently collected his accoutrements.

Defeated, she tottered after him. 'How did you do that? Just tell me. I think I'm having a bloody breakdown.'

Lightly tapping the brim of his hat, he imparted a guileless smile. 'It was a pleasure making your acquaintance. I trust you will sleep peacefully tonight after the adjustments. It may take some while before you see the full benefit, or it could happen quite suddenly and all at once. I'll see myself out.' He turned briefly, eyes a blue twinkle behind those ridiculous glasses, miraculously reappeared. 'Twenty second of March, Mrs. Jellow. Around the same time if not a minute or so before. Merry Christmas.'

She watched helplessly as he opened her front door and stepped into the night.

1859
London

Mr. Ambrose Bind

A Small Meal in Deptford & Better Prospects

Mr. Ambrose Bind sat devouring a meal of chicken and potatoes at a Deptford tavern. Having shredded the last morsel of flesh from the bird, he licked the grease from his fingers, took a long quench of ale and sat back with a sated grunt.

There'd been good lots at the victualling yard that morning: cocoa, salt beef, biscuits and even coffee. Not many bidding, so he'd got all he wanted.

Mr. Bind, a lugubrious man singularly devoid of outward pleasantries, was in his fortieth year and had been a widower for the last ten. He lived in a Clapham boarding house, and slept each night in a squalid room without companion. Rumour was that his only son had been pressed by the Navy and not been in communication since. Only he knew the truth of that. By accident or design, Ambrose was a man alone and unaccounted for.

Beyond the tavern's open window, the foggy river was blotted with steamers and barges. The filth of the city dwelled in this neighbourhood, and Deptford's fine churches could not cleanse its soul. Bloated corpses still fetched up on the beach and, like a foul disease, the stench of the Thames oppressed the mind of sinner and penitent alike.

Life varied little for him. Sometimes he was hired by bailiffs and took a meagre sum from any goods they cast off, but most days he could do little but scrape a pittance travelling and scavenging. Sometimes from the living, sometimes the dead: a miserable fee for moving a body cut down from the rope. There wasn't much Ambrose Bind hadn't seen, heard or smelled, and it was this wretchedness, and perhaps his own conscience, that had led him lately to the sanctity of the Church.

He stretched up and stamped his numbed feet on the stone floor. Gathering his coat, he made to leave the tavern. Tomorrow was an early start and promised to be both a blessing and a curse. His services were required in Portsmouth, a place more heathen than here, and one that dredged a particularly noxious stink.

Ambrose was to journey by second-class rail to the town, where he would meet a gentleman by the name of Purse, at an inn. The following day, Purse would hire a coach and accompany him and the goods on to Surrey. All this could not be achieved in a short time, so there would be separate accommodation, at the other man's expense.

The nature of the goods he'd to handle was as yet undisclosed. He was not one to probe into the business of others. Suffice to say, having previously been hired by him, Ambrose was satisfied that he was dealing with a generous, God-fearing man of considerable eminence. It would certainly be a day better than most. In that rare glimmer of optimism, he set off to collect his dray to make the journey home to Clapham.

2014
Christmas

A Happening in Twickenham
Payment Due & Duly Paid
A Trust in Hand
&
Promise Made

Sophie had been unusually decisive. She'd turned down her mother's invitation to Scotland, slammed in her notice at work and completed Christmas shopping, which included several packets of mince pies and two cases of wine. It was cheaper to buy in bulk.

Provisions stuffed in cupboards and plonked on messy surfaces, she took a bottle to the settee, and toasted to life without the toxic charm of Granny.

She awoke on Christmas Eve morning in a fit of bilious determination. After munching dry-mouthed through breakfast, she collected a roll of dustbin liners and thudded to the bedroom, assertion aforethought.

First, it was the bed. Diary back on the desk, cushions and pillows flung aside, sash thing yanked off, and stuffed into sacks. Then to the wardrobe. Mohair, silk and velvet scraped from their hangers, shoes hurled out, on and on, everything ruthlessly force-fed into black plastic, then humped into the hallway.

In the process of heaving the last spewing bag from the room, Sophie knocked into the bedside cabinet. A small red card flipped mid-air and landed at her right ankle, nestling like an affectionate cat. '*Gifford Hans. Mattress Turner. A personal service for the Promotion of Perfect Sleep*', it read. She snatched it up and looked at the back: *24/12* was inked in Prunella's smudgy scrawl.

Before the date could register, the doorbell gave three shrill and insistent blasts. She was still in her pyjamas. Card in hand, she dumped the sack in the wardrobe, collected a jumper off the floor and stomped to the door.

A tall figure stood motionless behind the bobbled glass. She crouched down and spoke into the letterbox. 'Yeah? Who is it?'

'Good afternoon. I have an appointment regarding Miss Prunella Flaggon,' a stranger's voice stated firmly.

'Don't know anything about it,' Sophie shouted, dragging the jumper down over her head. 'She's not here and I'm very busy.'

'Madam, forgive me. I am Mr. Gifford Hans, mattress turner. The appointment for noon today was made some time ago. It may have slipped your mind,' the voice suggested.

Sophie consulted the card and saw *12 o'clock* dashed in biro at the bottom. 'Oh, really?' Kicking aside a pile of letters, she tugged at the latch and wrenched open the door. A blast of freezing air stung her skin. 'I'm not Prunella,' she said.

A tall, thin man as old as Granny stood before her. Ramrod straight in coat and hat, he possessed what Prunella would have described as 'good bearing'. He looked perished.

She said, 'I don't even know what the time is.

Suppose you better come in,' and, watching him step onto the mat, slammed the door shut behind them.

As he painstakingly brushed the weather from his coat, rested his hat on the brass umbrella stand and placed his walking stick beside it, she wondered how long he intended to stay.

Beneath the naked hallway light his hair shone silver-grey, his skin a luminous white but for tiny flares of crimson on each cheekbone. Peering over large square spectacles, his gaze rested on her with ineffable merriment. He gave a slight bow. 'A very good afternoon, madam. My apologies for disturbing you. I am here to attend to a mattress.'

She glanced at the card again, back at the bespectacled face, and curled her mouth in a sour smile. 'Oh, yeah, the mattress.'

'This is why I am here, at the appointed hour.'

A Granny joke, she decided. He doesn't know she's dead. 'Prunella isn't here,' she told him again, her back to the closed door, and showed him the card. 'I don't know what this is. Actually, my – '

'I am apprised of the sad circumstances.'

He sounded very formal, like a solicitor. She glanced down at the label on her inside-out jumper. 'Okay. I'm Sophie, her granddaughter. I'll show you.'

'Please, do not inconvenience yourself,' the man interjected once more. 'I am familiar with the arrangement.' He proceeded along the hall.

'Oh, you've been here before,' Sophie said, failing to recall any mention of him.

He went ahead, picking his way among the chaos and on into the bedroom.

She tagged behind. 'Typical of Granny. Always

planning stupid games; you probably know that. Bit late now, though, isn't it?' She pushed the wardrobe doors to, the vast bed between her and the old man. 'Been having a clearout. If I'd known before . . . '

Mr. Hans smiled and removed the spectacles, slipping them into his coat pocket.

From her visits with Granny to Savile Row, Sophie recognised the hand-stitching on that coat, the soft, fluid way the cloth moved and fell with each of his graceful movements. He was, in the way Prunella had been, elaborately elegant. Her mood thawed. 'So you're actually *this* Gifford Hans?' She said, and wafted the card again. 'Do you really turn beds?'

'I attend to mattresses, madam.'

Sophie looked at the mattress, then back at him. Even Prunella's most superhuman feats never involved such tasks. 'Aren't you a bit . . . ? This looks really heavy. I mean, I'm not fussed. You don't have to.'

Mr. Hans radiated the warmest and broadest smile, like unexpected sun melting a morning frost. 'Miss Sophie, your alarm is perfectly understandable, and your expression of concern very familiar to me. It is to be expected, given the nature of my endeavours, for clients to have a natural expectation of a younger man, or these days, woman, employed to execute the task.'

Despite herself, Sophie giggled and slouched across the bed.

'I must continue.'

She jumped back. 'Sorry."

As the old man's gaze swept across the muddle of duvet and pillows, his expression darkened. Suddenly weathered by years, that generous smile shrank to a disconsolate thread. 'You do not sleep here,' he uttered with startling force. 'You have not slept in the bed.'

'So what? I never asked for it.' She jabbed an accusing finger at the urn sitting on the desk. 'Or that.'

The man stayed silently stationed at his post, frail hands like leaves wintering on his chest, eyes now corpse-grey.

Sophie crossed to the window and pulled back the curtain. 'I don't know why she gave me all this. Now I've got to live with it.' She stared out into the garden. 'And no one liked her, you know. She could be so vile. That memorial thing was gross. Horrible. My mother didn't even go, that's how much she hated her.'

A cool light glistened on her round crumpling face. 'I got used to all the insane things she did. But I mean, mattress turning? Fancy sending an old man round just to wind someone up.' Glancing around she saw the visitor was leaving and padded after him into the hallway. 'Sorry, didn't mean that. Hey, do you want a drink? I could do with one' She gestured to the middle room. Mind you, it's a total pigsty in there.'

Mr. Hans didn't move. In that confined space, she thought maybe he'd drawn too close her, but he lowered his head in solemn reflection, like a headmaster about to give an appraisal on a student's progress.

'Apart from minor and unavoidable adjustments to follow, the mattress is now thoroughly turned. I promise, madam, you will find the benefits transformative.'

Sophie, suddenly wearied by her strange visitor, flopped helplessly against the wall. 'Turned? You haven't – I mean, you *are* joking?'

'My client left a small fee for the service.'

Her toes itched. 'Client? Oh. Well, if Granny owes you anything, I've got money.'

'Your kind offer is sadly unacceptable. The debt belongs to the previous incumbent and is not yours to settle,' the old man insisted, his voice tightening. 'Therefore I must prevail upon you to find the fee. It is a requirement.'

'What debt?' Sophie shut her eyes, as if the world may become clearer if she couldn't see it. The creeping, enervating fear was back, a self slipping back to incoherent ways. Her mind tracked recently observed moments. Then: 'I remember.'

Back in the bedroom, she snatched the ripped wallet from the desk and brought it to him, trembling out a folded bundle of notes. 'Is this what you mean?'

'Indeed. The efficacy is incalculable.' The mattress turner reached into his coat pocket. 'Shall we make a new appointment?'

'What for?' Sophie's mind dwindled further, a shadow of disappearing thoughts. Her fearful mood was gone and she was drawn to the details of his clothing once more. Where was he going? After all that had passed between them, whatever that was, he was leaving. 'It is Christmas Eve,' she reminded him, a trifle petulant.

'Madam, please forgive me for detaining you at such a time.'

'The trains stop early tonight. You don't have to go.'

She trailed after him as he negotiated the

passageway, the light around them dimming. The old man gathered his walking stick from the stand. By the time he'd reached for his hat, he was as dull as a grey moth fluttering noiselessly in the impossible distance.

Sophie strained her eyes at the murk, a heavy, toxic stench of paint burning her throat. The air, now dusty and dank, clung to her skin. She coughed and pinched her face to keep awake, eyes fixed ahead.

Shade by shade the grey lifted and the faint beacon that was Mr. Hans reappeared. Its glimmer grew brighter until, like a constellation of stars, it exploded onto the pitch black. Captured in the halo of dazzling light he froze, his face mask-white, coat now a showman's cloak. Then, with an extravagant flourish of his hand he bowed so steeply, Sophie thought she heard the swish of velvet. And he was once more swept into darkness.

She grasped at the vanishing image, but stumbled, falling clumsily against the door.

A touch on her hand, whether to hinder or to aid, was so icy it burned. The shock bolted from head to toe.

Sophie stood upright, shielding her eyes in the glare of the electric bulb, mind neatly contained.

Mr. Hans, wearing his glasses, hat set firmly on his head, reached for the door. Twisting the latch, he eased up the swollen wood and opened it onto the night sky.

She said, 'How long have you been here?'

He stepped into the frosty and deserted road. Turning quickly, he lifted his hat and smiled. 'It was a pleasure to make your acquaintance at last. Until the next time, madam, I bid thee perfect rest.'

In the bedroom, Sophie gathered the duvet and the pillows neatly piled at the foot of the bed, without daring to think how they'd arrived there, or where the time had gone. As she dutifully arranged the bedding across the mattress, a small burgundy satin label at the foot caught her eye: *Glee & Sons. Purveyors of Fine Beds and Furnishings. Established 1859.* Next to it rested a yellowing piece of paper, with several numbers written in a precise, close hand: *Turn number: 30362. (Former occupation): 240 (New): 1. Adjustments to follow. H. P.*

1950

Expectations of Twickenham
&
An Unwanted Arrival

In 1944 the Germans dropped a bomb on a Twickenham road, precisely eliminating a terrace of three houses.

Over six years later, a gummy space still grinned where the doomed properties had once stood.

The other historic and unfortunate feature to this otherwise unassuming road was its baldness. Apart from the display of greenery found in the tight front gardens, the road was treeless. They were planted in other roads on the estate but in this one, a committee of residents decided that due to the mess caused by falling leaves, they would not have trees.

Those parsimonious and short-sighted folk may live to see flats built over the bombsite, but they would not be around to witness future residents' dismay at the lack of foliage.

Until now, these were the only two things worth commenting on.

'Is this it?' Prunella enquired, leaning across Benjamin and pushing open the car window. 'No wonder you forgot. I cannot recall a house or a place so dreary.'

They were sitting in Mr. Glee's 'glorious' new motor car: a Jaguar saloon, its opulent presence in shameless contrast with the terrace of plain, dumpy maisonettes on view.

There was a private entrance for each flat, and Prunella accepted the dull, grubby sheen of the lower door from the perspective of a long view. Lives change and so do doors. A pot of paint would do it. At least for a door.

Benjamin cast a nervous glance at his passenger. 'I did once deliver to a good address near Richmond Park, but I got to admit, here don't look too salubrious.' Leaving the car, he rounded to the passenger door and swung it open. 'But you wait to see what they done on the inside, little hen.'

Prunella swept from the car and smoothed down her velvet cape. 'I'm famished. We need fortifying before those men arrive.'

The good neighbours of that modest Twickenham street pressed against their respective windows, necks craned until the strange couple disappeared from mortified view. In the area's most respectable public house, patrons imbibing at its wide, circular bar, swivelled around and gawped shamelessly. The barman, noting Prunella's 'exhaustion' and her handsome companion's quality attire, ushered them both to a private room, but even he trailed a long, worried wondering in their direction.

'When this becomes riotously wicked and we are served more than the peasant fare, I think I'm going to enjoy my time here,' Prunella opined, over the basic meal of bread and cheese. 'It may not be easy for others, but for me I believe it will be an interesting period. And we must arrange for young Joseph to meet the offspring. That poor child needs more external influences. You are so hard on him.'

'You save that mollycoddling for your own. You've got a poor fella that loves you to hurt and dismiss. I feel for the lot of 'em.'

'Don't be silly, Mr. Glee. Borrowing is different. I'd be hell to live with. I'll let him go. Call it a merciful release.'

Luncheon over, the pair returned to the address to find the removal van arrived and the men preparing for work.

Prunella pattered after her companion into her new home, damp and gloom closing around her. 'Oh, dear, Mr. Glee.'

'It just needs a bit of living in. I'm sure they fixed it better than it was. Now go and take a look.'

She found the sitting room freshly painted, but it was cold and the boards still bare. She turned and followed the hall down to a middle room. This was a fair size, with an open fireplace and a side window overlooking a yard and a border of untended earth. The room led on to a small scullery, where a stove had been installed. In the deep pantry, shelves were bleached and scrubbed. Opening the back door, she stepped into a yard overlooked by all and sundry, neighbours' washing hanging from every post.

She lowered her eyes, a glitter of self-pity on the pale lashes. In the distance, a school bell rang, chased a few seconds later by the high shouts of children at play.

She returned to the hallway and waited as the men set down the last of the furniture. Benjamin went outside to issue further instructions regarding the bed.

First they brought in the decorative serpentine walnut headboard, followed by the footboard of similarly elaborate style. Next the rails arrived with the carved supports. Finally, the men staggered in with the mattress, and the task of assembling the monstrous thing commenced. When the men left a while later, their faces were grey from exertion.

Benjamin met her frightened stare. 'I see you ain't so sure now. This quality always looks imposing on first viewing. The bed just needs a proper dressing. You'll get used to it. Before the week is out you won't want nothing less.'

She looked around. Walls were newly papered in cornflower blue; her desk was set beneath the open window and laid out with pens and paper as if it had always been there; a French gilt mirror was mounted on the far wall and her favourite curtains hung on the open window. All about her the sun blinked and fell in broken, honeyed light, yet she found no pleasure in it. 'If this is a punishment, Benjamin, you went to a lot of effort.'

'Punishment, is it? If that how you're fixed on seeing it,' he growled, dark eyes flashing. 'Ever since I known you the world must bend your way. I tried my damnedest never to raise my voice, when what your carrying on deserved was summat far stronger.' A curl of his black hair touched the ceiling's glass shade as he towered over her.

She didn't flinch. 'Brute force? How did that apple fall so near to the tree?'

'Whatever your cleverness means, we all took a bite at some time. So don't start the play-acting, 'cause you ain't the leading role no more.' He swung away to gather his effects, his hands shaking.

She followed him to the door, watching as he

slipped into the car, his back, a wall of prickling pride.

'Have a safe journey home,' she called, sweetly. 'And my best love to Joseph.'

He clicked open the quarter light and took a deep breath, steadying his tone. 'Righty-o, then. No more dramatics,' he warned, and raised a gloved hand. 'You know where Twigmere is.'

The school bell rang again, and the day fell silent. She eased back from the step, a wayward shadow capturing her face. 'I'm planting a tree in this wretched place,' she called, her voice trembling over the stolid quiet. 'Planting a tree, for next time, my dearest friend.'

He closed his eyes. Not the first nor last keeper of that ancient Surrey custom, Mr. Benjamin Glee sighed at its unfathomable and needless complications.

He turned the ignition key. 'I'll give you dearest friend,' he muttered. Despite himself, he smiled and, comforted by the deep growl of the engine, he moved off. 'Next time, ye gods. Well I done what I had to. Call it an investment or your merciful release. I'll be long gone when that time comes.'

Until then, and possibly after, life goes on and on without release, along with its investments.

1859
Portsmouth

Ambrose

An appointment & a Change of Agreement

The weather was fine and the sky a nursery-rhyme blue when Mr. Ambrose Bind, crumpled in best flannel overcoat, stepped down from the train. He glanced at the station clock, noting that he was still in good time; it was over an hour before his meeting with the gentleman.

The journey by train had been cramped, loud and very long. He'd been drawn into conversation with a man who had recently travelled to Peterborough. From the lavish praise of its great cathedral, plus the excellence of the railway, Ambrose was minded one day to visit – although another traveller remarked there was little else to enjoy in the place, and Lincoln's church was finer.

'What about Winchester's and that be closer?' someone else chimed in. At an unexpected delay at Havant, all agreed that no train could ever be relied upon to reach any cathedral in any part of the land.

Now thankfully arrived, Ambrose stamped his swollen feet and took three long gulps of the sea air. Removing a small knife from his pocket, he studiously curled out the worms of grime beneath his fingernails.

Following the gentleman's instructions, he strode at

a leisurely pace towards Southsea. He wandered the streets, alerted to the fine villas with their elegant balconies and the expensive glazing – for Mr. Bind was not without discernment. 'Rich pickings here, away from the wretches and the filth,' he muttered. 'Pity I can't be making more benefit of my time.'

In the distance, the Solent shivered beneath bright sunlight and his thoughts swung back to the memory of his long departed boy – a momentary wrench, then a veil drawn down and memory swiftly dismissed, he proceeded to the inn.

Ambrose entered the premises and on into the saloon with an assured swagger. As instructed by his bountiful employer, he gave his name to the bartender. He was thus directed to a table, where, in short time, he was served beef broth, two good cuts of bread and a tankard of ale.

After his meal, suffused in a glowing sense of uncharacteristic well-being, Mr. Bind settled back and surveyed the inn's accommodation. It was decent enough for admirals and merchants and of greater intrigue than he'd first supposed. Shadowy corners, low doors and, to his surprise, a deep well. Secret passages held their dark tales there, he fancied – a hole, where kings and priests took refuge in olden times. And then Ambrose thought of his own secrets. He'd never before been to a place that caused such imaginings.

The clock had long since passed the hour, and he began to fret. It was already dusk and within the saloon, guests, returned from the steam packets, were now retiring to their accommodation, while others prepared for the early evening crossing. More faces appeared, sightseers for new ship, but still the gentleman was nowhere in sight.

A deep melancholy aggravated Ambrose's mood. Soon it would be night, trapped with all the horrors of the place, not to mention the history of this godless town to haunt him. He could not escape. If his patron did not appear, what was he to do but pray that he would not be murdered for the clothes he wore?

Barely had he succumbed to hopelessness, than a light touch rested upon his arm. A young boy stood trembling before him, worrying at the cap in his hand. 'Sir, are you Mr. Ambrose Bind?'

'I am.'

'A gentleman by the name of Purse, sir, asked me to escort you to his rooms.'

Ambrose grunted in relief and bundled up his coat. He followed the boy upstairs and along a maze of corridors until they came to the door.

The boy stopped outside, and put a finger to his lips. 'Go straight in, sir,' he whispered and fled without a sound.

Apart from a small lamp flickering weakly on a side table, the room was in darkness and breathlessly still. Ambrose could just discern the bent shape of the elderly gentleman. He stepped forwards and bowed. 'Mr. Purse,' he whispered, peering into the gloom. 'Asking your pardon, there was some delay.'

As if sensing his guest's unease, the gentleman turned the gas a little higher. He raised a frail hand, cautioning silence.

The large room was comfortably furnished with two chesterfield couches, a desk, chairs and, to Ambrose's astonishment, a cradle festooned in white lace. He stepped a little closer, conscious of his heavy tread across the floor. 'I do not understand, Mr. Purse, are you . . ?' His enquiries were curtailed by the helpless wail of a young baby. Ambrose stepped back, his eyes searching the room for a maternal presence.

'I trust your journey was uneventful, Mr. Bind,' the gentleman uttered softly, moving to the desk. He gestured to the now quieted crib. 'Do not be alarmed. For this is not the worst of your consignments. I am certain far more onerous tasks have befallen you.'

Ambrose pawed nervously at the overcoat across his arm. 'Mr. Purse,' he begged, incredulous, 'a child? What business do I have with the mite? You are most kind, but this ain't for the likes of me.' The scavenger lowered his eyes. 'Sir, I am become a religious man of late. I have never asked before of your private business.' He faltered. 'I done some strange work, but I never took an infant in my charge. Begging your pardon, sir, I cannot do the thing.'

Glancing up, he saw the old man's blue eyes glinting in the gloom, an expression of derision more withering than any words. A low humming filled his ears. Like the flow of ink spilt, the tune quickly spread. Seeping black tendrils shaped and wormed their witless lullaby into Ambrose's mind. He shook his head vigorously, trying to dislodge the noise. Reaching for a chair, he stumbled clumsily against the wall. The humming ceased. 'An orphan, I'm presuming, sir, and you the kindly guardian seeks my willing aid.'

Mr. Purse was now seated at the desk, squinting at him through a monocle. 'I have arranged lodgings, and bedding. Food will also be provided. I trust all will be satisfactory. And here you will find . . .' He nodded to an envelope lying on the scriver.

Ambrose's eyelids flickered in fevered calculation; he sighed expectantly.

The old man took up the envelope and pushed it towards him. 'A little remuneration above the initial fee for the unexpected nature of my commission.'

'Commission, eh?' thought Bind. 'Please, sir, if I may trouble you and make enquiries?' His voice thick with gratitude, he asked, 'The poor orphan, be it a boy or girl? If I may know, for my conscience, to be familiar in case anything should occur.'

'And what thing could possibly occur that may prick your conscience, Mr. Bind?'

'I'm sure I do not know what you mean.'

Once more, the tiny plaintive cry caused Ambrose to flinch. From the corner of his eye, he detected a slight figure emerge from the enveloping shadows.

Even through the murk, he sensed the creature's mystic beauty: hair twisting at her white shoulders, her graceful movements as she noiselessly approached the crib and gently lifted the child. When she tilted her face toward the old man, he witnessed the faintest smile pass across those startling features.

Later, as he lay in his sheets, Ambrose contemplated the bewitchment he was drawn into, of the infant and the old man. Finally, his mind rested upon the marvel of the woman's smile as it was directed towards the gentleman. It had been a communion of the deepest friendship, its nature found only after decades, if not lifetimes, of companionship.

January 2015
Hertfordshire

Lydia

Beneath Her

An hysterical Mrs. Jellow fled to London après the mattress turner's visit and spent Christmas at a friend's house. All the home-making and other decorative excesses were messing with her head. What Lydia needed was therapy, of another kind.

'I think I'm going mad,' she confided, her nose stuck in a glass of hefty Shiraz. Not a word had been mentioned about her visitor. He didn't seem real now, but other, apporting things, still troubled her.

She spent long hours talking around what kinds of extreme behaviour a person is capable of when under the influence of, say, drink, or anxiety and whether these actions count. 'I mean, you're not really yourself, are you . . . they?'

The opinion was that everyone is responsible for their actions, regardless. This favoured dissociative disorder, brought on by stress, was just an excuse used by psychopaths or nasty people to justify beating up their partners.

'Oh. I didn't do that.'

'What?'

'Nothing.'

And you simply do not know about an aged dotty husband's last desperate breath – whether it had been voluntary exhalation, or an emergency exit to get away from a wild-haired woman bearing down with an iron skillet.

And there was the mother. That ring, for instance. Lydia would've inherited the jewellery anyway, along with other treasures, but in these uncertain times, how can you trust underpaid nursing home staff? And the whole process had been taking so long. For every phone call summoning Lydia, there'd been the improbable and infuriating rally on her stubborn mother's behalf. She could've visited the home on that Wednesday, but ignored the call, assuming it was just another 'Nah, nah, nah, nah, nah! Up yours, grasping daughter.' But it was the genuine and final thing.

Lydia should really use the time to address her callous and mercenary nature. Instead she took the easier option and chose a Reiki practitioner, who wittered on about karmic leakage.

'Well, don't just stand there. Get a fucking plumber.'

Many a true word is said in jest.

Now, massaged by the slack embrace of lucrative alt. therapy, Lydia had arrived home to Herts. Were the shires her thing? With its constant self-rejoicing and depressingly long high street, even if it did have a well-respected store offering wine-tasting sessions, this manor was becoming a tad dull.

She triple-unlocked the door to her bijou home, stepped into the hallway and dropped her luggage with an appreciative sigh. She wrinkled her nose: lavender oil, camphor – that newly cleansed aura suffusing the place with fragrant talisman. Her eyes rested on the gorgeous De Morgan wallpaper. What a comfort good taste was; she could always rely on herself in that department.

Discarding her shoes en route, she sauntered into the front room and pressed at the window. It was lovely; even the minuscule back garden looked cute. Such a shame it was in the brain dead sticks. She wandered back to the hall to scoop up the post.

It was there among the handful of cold, damp letters. Did Lydia really expect him to disappear?

The card not so much fell as dive-bombed and glowered up at her, red as blood. She stepped over the intrusion and returned to the front room and plunged into the sofa. Now what was it about karma? She didn't believe it anyway, and slapped the post down on the sofa arm.

Onto the kitchen where, ignoring the table with the rings, she opened the massive fridge. She wasn't hungry after all. Coffee? Perhaps give that a miss today. She left the kitchen and made her way upstairs.

Halfway up Lydia began her deep breathing: one, two, three. She entered the room, her eyes half closed until it felt safe enough to look.

The bed was stripped and the linen folded in a tidy pile on the blanket box, exactly the way it had been left. She'd not set foot in the room that dreadful night and, seeing it in the stark light of reason, neither had that evil old bespectacled charlatan.

She began to dress the bed, but with reverence, as if it she were preparing a corpse for its final outing. A light dusting of talcum powder and then the sheet: a sail of sinless, crisp white cotton set it on its way. Guiding and smoothing, her hand brushed across the raised manufacturer's label – and something else she'd missed – a papery, crinkling thing. She peeled back the sheet. On the talcumy mattress sat a yellowing scrap of card. It was like those address tags on old-fashioned suitcases, even the type a child evacuee would carry on their person during the war, or worse. Lydia fingered the tag, stroking the small, close writing, her legs shaking. 'Oh, my God,' she squeaked. 'How in God?' and read: *Turn: 1 (This occupation):1 Adjustments to follow. H. P.*

'Is this you, Mamma? You've come back to haunt me.' And she crashed onto the mattress, the sheet with its five hundred threads to the inch rising like spectral wings around her.

2015
Twickenham

The View from Here and There

The cosmic like intervention of Christmas Eve had left no trace. Several days later, Sophie was propped on that spindly Arts & Crafts chair, in need of another happening.

The phantasm that was Mr. Gifford Hans had been swept from memory, incidents of magical transportation replaced with a jaundiced recollection of her only visitor: an old bloke who came around to drone on about beds.

She stretched up and peeled from the chair's rush seat. A shower of crumbs and sweet wrappers rained onto the already encrusted carpet.

In the freezing bathroom, she found a toothbrush and scrubbed at her wine-stained teeth. After showering, accomplished with her eyes shut, she dripped to the dining room and turned on the gas fire. She fumbled out some damp clothes from beneath the table, and began to dress. A weak winter sun caught her reflection in a long mirror, and winked. 'Fuck off!' she growled, which was unlike her, and threw a towel at the thing.

She sloped, fully dressed, the few feet to the kitchen and bolted down a couple of stale mince pies. Lassitude once more overwhelmed her and it was back onto the settee. Lulled into its welcoming miasma, she curled up, her gaze drifting to the window. Outside, the leafless branches of the magnolia tree swayed against the lightening sky – a shiver of green buds tangling in that slow dance. Even in the densest, deepest winter there seemed to be signs of spring. Drawn into this revelation, Sophie saw, for the moment at least, how surprising she could be.

That alien perception stirred, its palette lighter. Like winter itself, she slept – resurrection toiling unseen.

Railway engineering works at Twigmere were a problem over the Christmas period. Customers travelling to London were advised to reconsider their journey.

Young Ben Glee found reconsidering or any deviation from routine a challenge. This inflexibility had stood him in good stead in regards to commerce.

He was the most suitably educated and temperamentally disposed of all the Glees to make a success of the family business. Admittedly, Great-great-grandfather had been very successful in his day, but that had been haphazard, reputedly by brute force and tyranny. Others had also made an excellent contribution, but even they had ultimately wandered from the path. Courteous, dedicated Ben, on the other hand, was proving more than equal to any of his predecessors in that ruthless trade of bed selling.

In more nuanced areas of life such dry diligence had proved of little use.

After visiting his elderly mother the evening before, he'd planned his route from Surrey to Middlesex.

With an early start that morning, and despite long delays at Woking, he arrived at Twickenham in comfortable time for his appointment. He consulted his map for the address and decided to go the rest of the way by foot. Following the railway line, he walked briskly to the next station, with a good half an hour to spare.

He found a small café and sat regarding the cheery outlook. Glee's should do well in somewhere as smugly well-heeled as this. It was surprisingly leafy and pleasant for a London suburb – not a patch on Twigmere, obviously.

He reached into his pocket and pulled out a diary, flicking to the last page. December thirty . . . His heart plummeted. He focussed swimming eyes on the unposted letter before him. How could such a crucial thing be overlooked? This was appalling. All the preparation and he'd missed that? It was unheard of. He consulted the date and time. That, fortunately, was correct, and the surname? It must be Flaggon.

Ben checked his watch, swallowed the last mouthful of sweet tea and left the café in a state of high agitation.

The road was easy enough to find and he slipped the business card from an inside pocket and opened the gate. Unsure, he selected a grubby door on the right, and gave its bell three sharp rings and stepped back.

At first Sophie thought the bell was the alarm clock for work. And then remembered she didn't have either. She lurched upright, those holy revelations of earlier vanished. 'Oh, bugger.' Yanking the T-shirt over her belly, she plodded groggily to the hall and dived straight to the letterbox. 'Who is it?' And couldn't decide where the *déjà vu* began – the doorbell or her next statement? 'She's not here.'

A voice at her ear. 'Hello. Is this Sophie?'

It got that bit right. 'Yeah, who are you?'

'Good morning,' it continued nasally. 'My name is Ben Glee of Glee's Bedding. I am here to see how Christmas Eve went.' It coughed. 'Unfortunately, I omitted to send the follow-up appointment and as we have no telephone number on record, I wonder, is it convenient for you to spare a few moments?'

Sophie raised herself, and put her hand to the latch, lolling there, head resting against the freezing glass. Nothing was convenient. Yanking open the door, she took an involuntary gasp of post-Christmas air.

Her caller jumped to attention and presented a card, fluttering it nervously. 'Hello. We haven't met. I'm Ben, the manager,' he said, offering a gloved hand.

I'm not letting him in, Sophie decided, ignoring the hand. 'How did you get my name?'

'From our previous client, madam.'

This was also sounding familiar.

'We at Glee's like to meet our new clients personally,' he began. 'We pride ourselves on being ambassadors for the finest bespoke beds and promoters of perfect slumber – ' His little speech seemed to dry up.

Sophie bumped against the doorframe affecting a new-found 'dream on, buster' attitude. 'Someone came the other day. He didn't do anything.'

Her caller was undeterred by this. Clearly relieved to get a dialogue going, his voice brightened. 'Yes, I have heard of this before. In fact, he, Mr. Hans, does far more than you think. Far more. It isn't the actual *turning*.' Docile brown eyes rolled upwards in search of the correct phrase. 'It's a case of gradual adjustment. Imperceptible, I understand, at first. But you are quite happy with the service?'

'What service?'

The eyes were troubled. 'Christmas Eve? The appointment with our mattress turner?' he pleaded, panic edging into his tone. 'Here is my – ' Once more the card was offered.

Sophie's gaze drooped. 'That's not your name.'

'Er, no. This is Mr. Hans's card. He was the man who visited you on Christmas Eve.' At this point, the caller, his expression drained of hope, prepared to leave. 'I can see that I've disturbed your busy day. It only remains to say that I am extremely happy you will be taking over the, erm, terms of our highly valued client. Well, thank you for your time, Ms Flaggon. It *is* Ms Flaggon?'

'What terms?'

'In the sad the loss of your – '

'Are you talking about my grandmother?'

'Please accept my belated condolences.'

'What for? She was ninety-eight.' Sophie bumped herself from the doorframe. Jerking out her hand in a flipper like gesture she plucked the card poking from his fingers, and folded it into her arms and stared at him. At this point, she might have said, 'Now piss off,' but it would have been completely out of character.

The visitor presented a brave smile and dragged the gate shut. 'Almost a centenarian,' he said. 'I trust Mr. Hans will send a new appointment. Thank you, madam, and a Happy New Year.'

Sophie stepped barefoot into the garden and watched him amble away. What the hell was that all about?

She rubbed her fingers across the surface of the card and looked at it. It reminded her a lot of a little red satin thing somewhere around. Returning to the relative warmth of the hallway, she kicked the door closed behind her.

Crouching at the letterbox, Ben felt a tug at the door, and jumped up. A pasty-faced, dumpy woman of about thirty and thrown together in a few un-ironed clothes scowled up at him. Surely, he thought, this wasn't the relative of a woman the mattress turner had held in such high esteem. He was surprised by the state of the property, too.

It would have been nice to have met the original client. Ninety-eight? Pity the old woman didn't make it to a hundred. Her granddaughter, he presumed, was behaving like a sulky teenager. To think that Mr. Hans had extended his service to someone so unsuitable. It was hard to imagine someone as rude as her joining the ranks. Ben considered that last thought again. What ranks? Anyway, there was no benefit in persisting. She'd taken the card. Best thing now was to find somewhere to have lunch. Walking away, he sensed her eyes on him, and looked back.

She stood in the small front garden, her face raised to the winter sky. Placing the card he'd given her against her lips, she began to sway – limbs loose, invigorated and her face alive with childlike joy.

Ben turned and walked briskly to the station, troubled by what he'd seen. No time for lunch. He must return to Twigmere, update the entry or create a brand new one just for her. Why it concerned him so much, he had no idea.

1859
Twigmere

A Miss is as Good as a Mile & What's in a Name?

Some weeks had passed before Benjamin Glee opened the stranger's testimonial.

He'd been unsure about how best to explain the mysterious events to his young wife, without implicating himself. In the end, he decided that no explanation was required.

'A gift, no matter what it is and how it comes should be accepted with thankfulness and without question,' he told her. 'This be hope that we both must cherish.'

For him, the letter was the endorsement, the signed deed. The benefits of that curious arrangement, which no sane mind dare dwell too long upon, was theirs by guarantee. But the shopkeeper was curious to discover the name of his unexpected benefactor.

When at last the seal was broken and the now damp bonded paper reverently eased from the envelope, Benjamin was suddenly stung by the memory of his terrible confession.

He sat with his wife, a woman frail beyond her twenty two years, in their large, draughty sitting room. The fire burned low in the grate, and behind them the stony November sky pressed against the naked windows.

He put the letter near the lamp, his hands trembling. 'It says here, wife,' and very slowly he read the few lines. *To whom this letter may concern.* It began. *It gives me great pleasure in writing this testimonial of Her Majesty's Servant whose industry and loyalty has proved an extraordinary service within this Household.*

Benjamin glanced to the top of the page to make certain of that household, and continued. '*I forswear my* . . . here the words ran into each other and were too difficult for him to decipher. He picked up further along '. . . .*will provide all that is required from an honourable person committed and sworn to the improvement and quality of perfect rest*'. He mouthed the words. *Notwithstanding the short distance of time His My Faithful* . . . then scrawl.

Here, Benjamin was anticipating a name. '*Gif* . . *Giff?*' He frowned. 'That be it?'

Mrs. Glee leaned nearer and reached for the letter. He pulled away. 'Get off, woman. I can't read this one. Get me the glass from the cabinet, quick.'

The wife went to a table and duly brought a magnifying glass. 'What name does it give?' she asked, inching nearer, and pulling her shawl closer.

'I can't make sense of the words, they're smudged. The name must be in it.' Benjamin waved the magnifier over the bottom of the letter, where the sentiment was extravagantly repeated: '*Hereby this miracle My Faithful. . .*' then an indecipherable blur: '*Giff*' and then a flourish and '*of*'. The reader faltered, then: '*Hanns* or *Hands.*' He laboured over the sentence, and gave up. 'Is that him, Hands? That ain't right for a name,' he said. 'I reckon it be *Hans.*'

'Foreign?'

'That's his name, Hans.'

'First or last?'

'Last *or* first.'

'Maybe it says gift, Benjamin,' his wife suggested, timidly. 'You did say of one coming.'

'That ain't it. That be a name. Giff. Giffof, maybe not an f. I find it too like a d. Giffod, then.'

His wife was still unsure. He squinted at the words again and, refusing be contradicted, said, 'It be Hans Giffod. It can be made round the other way if it don't fit.'

And with the best or the worst will in the world, when the couple were received of their precious benefaction they sent in their finest country burr gracious thanks to Mr. Gifford Hans via his agent, Ambrose Bind, who was in no mind to disabuse them.

And as no one was ever told otherwise the 'gift of hope' was brought up as their own, and they called him Jacob.

Twigmere

A Trick of the Dark

Mr. Gifford Hans finished polishing Monday's glasses, and placed the large square frames on a table and rested back in his chair. His eyes wandered above the window to the ceiling, and traced the ominous outline of a deepening crack down the wall: subsidence.

Rising from his seat, he crossed to the fireplace and reached for the clock. His fingers hovered above the glass face, but this time hesitated and withdrew. He turned restlessly and moved to the door, but instead of opening it, his ancient frame melted into the wood, folding like a beam of sunlight against solid form. Then he and everything in the room was snuffed out and all was black.

Gradually, as if a witness to this strange happening were regaining consciousness, familiar shapes began to unfold from creases of emerging light. The mantelpiece, along with its clock, reappeared, redrawn into existence by that once obliterating hand. The window, hitherto naked, was now garlanded in brocade and lace, and pools of early sun scooped on its narrow sill. A small fire burned in that once blackened grate. Then, delicate as painterly lines may blossom on canvas, a female form was born.

She cast her eyes around the room as if seeking ways to make it more hospitable. Perhaps the table manifesting by the window was the thing she sought.

Bread and a jug of wine were soon set upon the pale oak. Was she expecting guests?

The woman stood tiptoe on dainty feet and reached up to accept a touch on her slender neck. Her companion, now shaped in flesh, held her in a long embrace. She led him to a low bed, where a tiny child lay.

The two bent over the infant in silent adoration, exchanging loving glances and laughing softly. At this point the ceiling cracked and tumbled; the scene collapsing in a furious gust of black smoke. Shared joy dispelled, precious moments evaporated.

Back on his chair, Hans lifted the glasses from the table and, holding them a few inches distant, perused a note from the young Mr. Glee. 'A new client,' he said to himself, nodding with approval. 'Excellent. This will save a lot of time and bother.' Glancing up at the clock, he noted the hand had not moved.

1909
Twigmere

Lineage Unknown
&
When a Man Chases After a Hat
&
Returns it Without Compromise

Mr. & Mrs. Jacob Glee had spent a pleasant day on the Isle of Wight. Glowing, if a little burned, from the late summer sun, they'd had a good crossing and now arrived back at Twigmere on the four-sixteen train from Portsmouth Harbour.

Clattering into the shop, Mrs. Glee propped her parasol next to the awning pole and sank onto a long sofa. 'I had a lovely time, but it is nice to be home,' she said, slipping off her shawl.

Mr. Glee remained by the door, checking the lock, making a show of rattling and banging the catch. 'This is coming loose, Minnie. Best get it changed. What with everything else, God forbid if the worst was to happen and insurance wouldn't pay.'

Minnie nodded, a troubled glance lingering over the crowded shop. Iron bed-bases and newly delivered furniture still in the brown wrapping were set without order on the bare boards. 'This place do need a tidy. Only after a day the dust is thick.' She patted the sofa's deep cushions. 'Anyway, shop's all yours now. You can have in what you like, do as you please. Change locks and all.'

Jacob walked over and sat beside her, removing his cap. He gave the peak a sharp flick. 'Not with him here watching. No matter what I get in new, it seems to stick.'

'Well, he did have a magic touch with selling, I'll give the old beggar that much.' She stood and brushed a hand across Jacob's hair, pressing her lips to his warm forehead. 'I can't believe at his years he'd have the energy to meither us what works all hours. Like your poor mother did.' Her voice lowered, delicately traversing unsure ground. 'Our Benjamin's got a way with selling. The boy's not bad, even of he do break a heart or two. He could give you more of a hand in the shop. That's if you've a mind to let him.'

Jacob got to his feet, and paced to the window.

She moved to the door of their private flat. 'Now you go and have a cogitate, my love, and I'll make us some supper.'

Jacob waited until he heard her tread on the stairs and then slyly returned his attention to the lock. Again he tapped the metal, felt around the latch, and then, setting on his cap, tugged open the door. The little bell gave a telltale ring. 'Won't be long, Minnie,' he called, and stepped into the street.

Except for carts being cleared after the day's market, Twigmere was quiet, the sun low, shadows nesting between the houses. The few children still at play rolled their hoops near to home, waiting for the bedtime call. One or two regulars from the local hotel weaved across the dappled view, giving an absent nod to a passing neighbour.

He trudged in the growing stillness, his mind wrapped in thought.

Unsurprisingly, Jacob was unlike any Glee before him, with neither his father's dark looks nor his ruthless ambition to match. And he could not marvel at the anomaly of his own son's freakish affinity to the Glee line, because he knew no better.

He was an unassuming, mild-mannered man, whose only dream was to be a signalman. But he'd been bound to the family business with no chance of escape to country railway cottages, or any other bucolic retreat. Now at the age of fifty two, Jacob had taken over that business. It was doing badly and the old man's constant meddling made the running of it even more of an upward struggle.

To make matters worse, big stores were opening and soon he and his wife would not be able to survive. Yet despite this, he resisted his fashionable son's constant prodding to move with modern times.

He plodded on, turning over his worries. On reaching the brow of a steep hill, he leaned back against the iron railings to admire a row of tiny cottages, their hanging tiles glowing pink in the setting sun. His gaze wandered away and up the curling hill to other timber-framed dwellings. Twigmere was indeed a surprising place, he thought, with much to offer the stranger and native alike.

A sharp breeze made him shiver. The pale sun squeezed through a gathering cloud, its failing rays combing the hill in an eerie light. The wind was picking up, rustling among the trees and, as if the season had switched, the temperature dropped. He turned back for home.

Below at the foot of the hill, a figure moved gradually toward him, the tap-tapping of a stick echoing in the deserted street.

The figure was making such pathetic progress that Jacob soon reached him, and found a well-dressed gentleman of some decrepitude. He was about to offer assistance when a sudden gust of wind lifted the gentleman's bowler hat and blew it across the street. Much to his astonishment, the hatless man leapt after the thing, chasing with great vigour as it rolled out of reach. Each time he came close the hat seemed propelled by some mischief and hurtled to another part of the street. It would have been comical but for the gentleman's evident distress.

'You wait there, sir,' Jacob called, 'it's got a mind of its own,' and took up the chase himself. He followed the hat, which now skirted and skittered beyond each grasp, and spent a good few minutes back down the hill and up again, before finally pouncing and seizing the item. 'I don't know if it be the wind or the hat what's got the devil in it,' he joked, waving it in the air. 'Here you are, sir. I hope it ain't too battered.'

The gentlemen approached him, his walking stick now pinned beneath his arm.

As the man received his bowler, Jacob took a sudden, backward step.

Everything else about the stranger's attire, for the shopkeeper had not set eyes on him before, was as to be expected for a gentleman. His greatcoat, although heavy for the season, was of the finest quality, his shoes hand-stitched. His features, if a little odd, were refined and the etched brow betrayed a studious nature. But his eyeglasses? They did not fit such bearing. Their bright garish blue was more Southsea funfair than Surrey evening. He was playing a prank on Twigmere dressed like that. A jester, or a lunatic.

The gentleman stood unabashed before him. 'You are most kind, sir.' Glasses removed he slipped them into a pocket. He peered closely at Jacob with the abandoned intensity of someone inspecting their property left in questionable safe-keeping. 'Very good,' he said, brushing down the recovered hat. 'I fear it may rain at any moment, and you are lightly dressed. Please, allow me to offer you something for your efforts, if only shelter from the elements.' The stranger gestured to one of the tiny cottages. 'I am just here.'

Jacob hesitated, the air now bitter as a winter frost.

The door to the cottage was already ajar. 'Do come in, sir.' The stranger beckoned. 'I have had a busy day and a young man barely left an hour past.'

Jacob crumpled off his cap and crept cautiously within.

The room was a peculiar and an unsettling shape; its only window was small and offered scant light. It was hardly the picturesque and welcoming cottage it appeared from the outside.

The gentleman was now crouched over the fireplace, adding papers and coal to the grate.

Jacob noticed an envelope on a small table. He squinted at it and tried to read the name.

'Please, take a seat.'

Startled from his prying, the shopkeeper looked up. The greatcoat was now gone and the gentleman sported a grey suit of unusually close cut and a pale yellow cravat.

'I'll stand, sir, if you don't mind,' Jacob mumbled.

'How is business, Mr. Glee?'

Jacob's skin tingled and his heart beat faster. Maybe, he thought, he is from the fair, a man playing mesmerising tricks and got me here to rob. Except I don't have nothing. 'You know my name, sir,' he said, 'but I don't remember you.'

The old man stepped back from the fireplace and smiled. 'Do not be concerned. I have a long acquaintance with our Mr. Benjamin Horace Glee. Still fit and interfering, as I understand, even at one hundred and one. You are his son, Jacob, and the new proprietor of Glee's.'

Jacob felt a wash of relief. 'Yes, sir. I took over a year back now. He still keeps a weather eye.'

'Quite so. And business thrives?'

'Truth be told, it ain't good,' the shopkeeper returned with unexpected candour. 'Nothing I do seems to . . .' He broke off. 'It's a curious thing, but I never seen you before. Must be a while back you knew him, sir. Before my time?'

'Indeed. I occupied a supplemental position. We will not have met.'

Those spears of clarity invoked in such unexplored circumstance pierced a distant memory. Something his father let slip in an absent moment, or was it a name he'd come across in old papers shuffled together in forgotten corners? And then it appeared before his eyes so clearly, it could have been written for him to read. 'Am I in the company of Mr. G. Hans?'

The man bowed. 'The very same. At your service, if you so wish it.' Once more he scrutinised the shopkeeper. 'I have a proposition, Mr. Glee. I believe it will prove of mutual benefit.'

At this, Jacob's mind began to work with an

unnatural alacrity. 'Benefit?' he said, reminded of recent and troubling details.

'Indeed. The large establishments are taking custom from the small traders, those reliant upon the loyal and local patron,' Mr. Hans replied, his voice weaving into Jacob's newly whirling thoughts. 'They steal an unfair advance on the traditional man. Their many agents seduce the public, and offer what shops such as yours cannot, and at a modest cost.' He allowed a moment for this to sink in. 'These new beds, especially, are proving very popular.'

The shopkeeper was already fastened closely on the words. 'We did well with beds once.'

'And now, Mr. Glee? Modern times, you see. It is enough to drive the little man working all the hours to bankruptcy. Or.' He glanced to the side and coughed discreetly. 'Fraud.'

The melodic tones now jarred in Jacob's ear. Why did the old beggar say that? What fraud could he know of?

'Mendacity borne of desperation,' supplied his strange host, as if dwelling in his mind. 'Invented calamity. Insurance claims of accidental fire. Even burglary. Quite fallacious, their misfortune wickedly contrived.'

The shopkeeper's guilty thoughts leapt to the shop's lock and its loosened catch. What wicked ideas were playing with him as his innocent wife sat worrying.

The old man's silvery words once more sliced into his doubts. 'Best unseat the big man at his game with a little audaciousness. I believe the vulgar parlance is 'get ahead.' And these new beds could do the trick.'

Jacob recalled Minnie's comment about his father's

magic touch. 'You reckon so? You reckon that'll do it?'

The old man began to pace back and forth like a prisoner maddened by the confinements of his cell. 'Most certainly. But there is a condition.'

'What'll that be?'

'These modern mattresses, popular they may be, have one considerable drawback.'

'They do?'

'Their cumbersome and unwieldy weight. They are heavy, Mr. Glee.'

Whatever internal or external connivance that made him balk at this last statement, Jacob's once racing mind braked, reversed and resumed its familiar sluggish pace. He hooked his thumbs in his waistcoat pocket and shook his head. 'I heard about them, Mr. Hans. Big, lumpy monsters. My son wants 'em but I ain't keen. What's wrong with the ones we got now, I say. And you can't move the blighters. How do folks budge 'em, let alone turn 'em to keep the things regularly aired?'

'Ah, you come upon my proposition,' the old man acknowledged with delight. '*They* have no need to turn them, for I provide such a service. Unique and bespoke. Glee's would be above all other establishments that do not, indeed, cannot offer such an irresistible convenience.'

The old man stood erect and appeared much taller than when Jacob had first encountered him. 'For I am a turner of mattresses. A personal service in the revolution of perfect sleep.'

The shopkeeper, his deliberations now slow as cheese, shook his head. 'Oh begging your pardon, sir.

No offence to you and the fine offer, but I wouldn't want to be getting wound up in new business connections. I'm not of a mind to. My wife and me likes to just get the stock in and sell it without complications.'

'Quite so. No complications.' Mr. Hans beamed. He directed his gaze to the corner of the room, where a small fire now glowed in the grate. 'I see I cannot tempt you with promises of prosperity, a business restored to heights beyond imaginings. You are not to be swayed by the prospect of rejuvenation from nights of flawless slumber; a life of extended vigour and longevity would hold no interest.'

By now, used to the gentleman's florid language, Jacob replied with ease, 'No, not for me. I never had it and never wanted all what you said. My old father stays with us now. None of his money did him no good, even though he does live on and on.'

The old man seemed amused by this assessment and a little relieved.

The room once mean as a grave began to thicken and fill with warmth, its wayward shape and brutal angles brushed by the mellow light.

Jacob yawned, his eyes heavy. 'Reckon I will take a seat, Mr. Hans, that is if you don't mind.' And he fell onto an upholstered chair.

The voice was distant and the shopkeeper wasn't certain where the singing came from or whose it was. A woman? The gentleman's wife? Too young. A granddaughter maybe. Perhaps it was his own dear mother humming a lullaby to her son. Could he remember that far back?

Mr. Jacob Glee, a man with no desire now, other

than to spend the evening with his wife. To listen to her talk of nothing as he drifted over memories of steam engines, gauges and the poetry of locomotives. Then to bed in the good old Staples, with the feather overlay and two eiderdown covers – to dream that dream of large rooms, gravely decorated and heavily curtained.

He heard snoring and opened his eyes.

Mr. Hans stood by the door. 'Your passion for the railways is unsurprising,' he remarked as Jacob wobbled to his feet.

'And the sea,' the shopkeeper said, reaching for his cap. 'I does like my trips to the Isle of Wight.'

'And so you ought,' Mr. Hans replied, closing the door behind him with a soft click.

The sun glistened on pavements wet from a recent shower and the sky was wiped of cloud. Jacob felt for his fob watch and saw it was almost ten past seven. He stepped from the canopy of a small cottage, where he'd taken shelter and walked briskly down toward the town and his waiting wife.

1859
Portsmouth

Ambrose has a Surprise

Ambrose awoke to a dull day and found himself fully clothed in a soft cot. He sneezed. On the opposite side of the room stood a washstand and a large jug and bowl. He sneezed again. Feathers.

Mr. Bind was not used to such comfort, and then he remembered. 'Lord save me, it be Portsmouth,' he said, the phantoms of the strange encounter with the old man beginning to re-emerge.

Over at the bowl, he splashed cold water over his face and sleeved away the filthy residue.

He groped around in his coat pocket and clawed out the coins. Surprised to see how much, he put his mind to the coming day. There was a nipper to deliver. Well-rewarded, but a queer business this.

Purse had ordered the carriage for eight, and it was already gone seven. Ambrose made his way to the saloon and took his seat at the window, staring out at the street. Already the place was busy with holidaying families, seamen and chandlers, no doubt the slopers taking cover in the crowds.

After a breakfast of eggs, mutton, half a tankard of ale, plus all the bread that would fit in his pockets, he made his way to the entrance to find Mr. Purse. Instead, he was met by the boy who'd taken him to the room the night before.

'Gentleman will be present shortly,' the boy

stammered, scratching his filthy head, cap raised towards the traveller.

Ambrose reached for his pocket, but gave himself a miserly caution and clasped both hands behind his back. 'Very good, he grunted.' Turning on his heel, he found his patron attired in mulberry cape and beaver skin top hat, approaching from a side door.

The old man commenced polishing his *pince-nez* on a silk kerchief. 'I trust you are rested, Mr. Bind.'

'Can't complain, sir.'

'And well fed?'

'Oh, yes, you are most kind,' Ambrose assured him, eyes flitting around for the cradle.

'The infant is without,' the gentleman said. Asleep since the sea crossing. It does sleep well.'

Bind waited for the carriage to draw up, and opened the door. He leaned in and found the cot cocooned in lace and resting unattended upon the plush upholstered seat. 'The lady, sir?'

The old man held him in a steady gaze. 'I believe you are confused. We travel without gentle company.'

'Am I to be alone with the mite?'

'Are you not familiar with children? My understanding was that you are a family man. I chose you as such.'

'I was, sir . . . but circumstances, Mr. Purse. They have had the better of me in regard to such matters. I ain't tended to an infant, since – It be a long time, sir.'

But the old man raised a gloved hand and directed the man into the carriage.

Within a short time, they were on their way to Surrey, the child still fast asleep.

2015
Hertfordshire

Enlightenment
&
Varying Views of a Small Cake

Of course, Lydia hadn't changed one bit. She'd chosen to dismiss the crinkly tag effect, putting it down to Christmas and nervous exhaustion. Meanwhile, the rings had been duly deposited beneath layers of wrapping paper at the bottom of a drawer, where they could never escape.

She sat shaving a cashmere jumper at the kitchen table. With each vexing bobble and snag, a new rationalisation presented itself. 'Considering everything that happened, I'm not that bad,' she whispered to the jumper. 'Not like some people I know. I make up for things in other ways. I reverted to the family name, out of respect to my mother. I didn't have to.'

Lydia's late mother had out-divaed even her. What with funnelling up the sympathy and allowances made by everyone, early life had involved so much eggshell treading that the household practically mastered the art of levitation. Not to mention the 'just be thankful, Lydia,' mantra. 'What your mamma went through, my God.'

What of Lydia's sibling? The sun had shone from his every orifice as far as the mater had been concerned. The younger brother, now forty-six, was in

New Zealand doing something in finances and Lydia hadn't spoken to him in years.

Papa Jellow had been a sweetie, but proved not long for this world – he was gone and buried before she was ten. He didn't leave much, either, which threw the mamma onto the mercy of doctors, tranquillisers and psychiatric wards. That's until Mamma found an alpaca-clad shoulder to cry on, which later turned out to have a bad case of the moth. 'Uncle' was a creep, even the brother saw that, and his tenure mercifully short.

Mamma got by. She liked the men and they loved her – a little gift here, a nice bit of jewellery there. Cars would draw up outside the house – more alpaca coats on the hallstand. And when quality shoes were safely squeaked upstairs, children found those unguarded pockets jangled with complicit rewards.

Hers, Lydia didn't include her brother in the suffering, was a childhood of unpleasant surprises, dirty strangers and uncertainty.

A warm tear wriggled down her cheek and rolled onto her hand. 'It's a fucking miracle I didn't turn out to be a criminal,' she consoled herself, fingers snipping that final unflattering blemish from the clothing.

It was all the childhood stuff forcing her to marry older men, a deep neurosis driving her to seek comfort in money and choose unsuitably sclerotic partners. Everyone said how enterprising she was, but so unlucky in love. And work. Why kill yourself, when you could get bread on the table. Didn't rely on state handouts, did she? No need, when wealthy men provided the same service.

Yet it was a leaky life, where love always trickled onto somewhere else. She gave a hicuppy gulp and her shoulders shuddered with genuine, heartfelt sadness. At least no one could call her a psychopath. They didn't feel or cry, psychopaths. That was a comfort and she reached for a tissue. Then that doorknocker gave the most distant and reluctant rap.

Ben was confident of his next follow-up appointment. The letter had been sent well before Christmas and, having met the woman, he knew what to expect. Despite meeting Mrs. Jellow again, he looked forward to spending a day in what Mr. Hans once described as a 'pleasing settlement of some antiquity'.

Arriving at Waterloo midday, he'd crossed London by bus and caught the train from Euston. He sank back in his seat and considered that morning's revelation.

Following his Twickenham encounter, Ben decided to create a new entry for Flaggon. It was that previous unsettling experience, perhaps, that prompted him to double-check this Jellow client.

Flicking the pages to the relevant date, he'd discovered Mrs. Jellow's new details had been added, and there they were again. The other addresses he'd seen before were also recorded below. Next to the addresses were dates, too, some going back years; however none corresponded to his own dealings with the client.

Here was yet another example of Mr. Hans's convoluted and eccentric method. Were there historic contacts between the old man and this client? Personal connections beyond her most recent purchase?

Unlikely, but it could not be ruled out. And why wasn't it mentioned? He tried to dismiss the puzzle, but it pressed on his mind throughout the journey to Hertfordshire. There was no time to think of it now; he'd arrived at Mrs. Jellow's most recent address.

Guiding his hand through an elaborate wreath of mistletoe and berries, he found a small brass knocker.

When Lydia heard that familiar rap, her mind, jumpy as a till roll, scanned the likely contenders. She wasn't expecting anybody.

Leaving her mending on the table, she skidded on stockinged feet down the polished hallway and into the front room. Whoever had knocked was leaving.

She minced to the window to view her escapee. A tallish, young . . . Ben Glee. Oh, Christ. He'd seen her. 'Hi,' she mouthed. And regretted it. Too late: he was turning on his heel and striding to her picket gate.

At the door, she met his sphinx like expression. 'Hi! You're from Glee's. Almost missed you.'

'Good afternoon, Mrs. Jellow. This is merely a courtesy visit.'

Confronting the aluminium-grey sheen of his suit, the rigidity of both hairstyle and manner, Lydia succumbed to the vision of a man-shaped metal sheet sliding beside her into the house. She blinked. 'Sorry, what did you say?'

'I'm following up with a courtesy call.' He looked momentarily distraught. 'You did receive our notification?'

'Oh, that,' said Lydia, recalling the letter-strewn grate. 'That was you? Again? You better come in. I just can't keep up with all these *gleeful* communications.' She turned and with a that-went-down-like-a-lead-balloon roll of her eyes, headed to the kitchen.

A sudden and sobering thought intruded into that teeming mind: the William Morris headboard. She'd looked up the price on those. Glee's wanted it back, or worse, payment. The sly bastards. Well, they weren't having it. 'We'll go in the kitchen,' she told him.

Down went the kettle switch, out came the cups. 'I've got a bone to pick with you, Mr. Glee.' In went the breath. 'Now don't take this personally, I'm not making any complaints about the bed, but you have some very strange people on your books and I'm not certain how far I'm going to take it.' Breath out.

Ben was crouched warily above the seat of a rickety cane chair.

'You can sit, it won't bite you,' Lydia said, stirring the coffee. 'I'm on a strict health programme, due to my nerves. This is decaf.' She brought the cup over to her visitor, now wedged in his chair.

'I'm sorry, Mrs. Jellow,' he said, eyes glazed, 'I don't understand. Books? We only employ the delivery men.'

'Who's this 'we'?'

He considered for a moment. 'Well, me, actually.'

'Thought so. And what about the coffin-dodger you sent to turn the mattress? What role does that crafty old bugger have in your establishment?'

Ben raised his eyebrows, drew in a deep breath of his own, and placed the cup on the flagstone tiles. He clasped his hands, agitation twitching in the trim fingers. 'I presume you refer to Mr. Hans. He is a rather mature gentleman. However, I can assure you, he is beyond reproach. I'm afraid I don't understand. Are you not satisfied with our service?'

Sensing she'd gone far enough, Lydia changed tack. 'All I'm saying, Ben, is that some very odd things happened. I can't mention what exactly as that would – well, to be honest, it's been bloody weird.'

Ben's face slackened with relief. 'Weird? Oh, yes, of course. Yes, yes, this is to be expected.'

'What is?'

'The results.'

'Results? He didn't *do* anything. Not what he was supposed to, anyway.'

The visitor pressed a hand across his chest in affirmation and prised himself from the seat. 'I heard this exact phrase only recently. It's not what you imagine. The benefits of a turned mattress can be both interesting and surprising. Let me explain.' He lifted his cup from the floor and respectfully placed it next to the sink. 'If I may. Our service is for the enhancement, the promotion of perfect sleep. There are elements, problems, perhaps, in our lives that require a little ironing.'

That fits, thought Lydia, half mesmerised by someone whose persona up to this point had been flattened by a steamroller.

'We don't realise how we are used to our little bumps and flaws. Only when we are offered something so perfectly formed do we then realise how, let's say, ill-shaped *we* have become. It's a chance to let go of our past, to redeem . . . This can be achieved through various interventions. It is different for everyone. The benefits can take some while, I understand, or be quite sudden and happen all at once.'

From across the kitchen, Lydia's hand slipped from the fridge and froze mid-air, clutching a miniature chocolate roll.

Ben was amazed at himself. All these lofty ideas unleashed. Words seemed to be raining down, information pouring into him and out, like a revelation. Epiphany. And this dreadful woman was listening to these words and taking note, he could tell, and yet here he was explaining what up to recently had been inexplicable to him: the role of the marvellous Mr. Gifford Hans.

Then, quick as a dream is stolen upon waking, the door to this evangelism and otherworldly insight was slammed shut. 'It is a question of adjustment,' he concluded quietly and looked round for the chair.

'Are you all right, dear? Here, have this.' Lydia, broken from the spell, offered him the cake and tenderly unpeeled its wrapper. 'And what about yours? You must have one of your own beds.' She parked herself on a stool opposite and, from force of habit, stuffed the cake into her own mouth.

Ben returned the query with a misty stare. 'No, I have an old Staples. It belonged to my parents.'

'And does he do it? Does Mr. Geriatric The Elder adjust *your* mattress?' she said, through a blur of chocolate sponge.

His eyes roved across a fragmenting memory. 'I don't believe so, as far as I recall.'

At the sink, Lydia rinsed some water over the cups. 'He did say something about coming back in March.

But until I know what that crap was all about, I really do not want him in my home. It is only a bloody bed, you know. There is nothing magic about a bed. Or sleep. Why do I need someone to come here and leave freaky things?' She turned to face him, a little drama in the move. '*You* tell me how he can be downstairs with me *and* upstairs putting tags on the bed. I mean, how else did they get on there?'

'Tags?'

'You know, ticket, label things? Sort of thing you get on old suitcases.'

'How many?'

'One. Why, do you owe me already? Anyway, it had lists of numbers. I threw it away.'

'Numbers?' Once again Ben was nonplussed. 'I'm certain there's a reason. They could be from another, er . . . One of your many moves,' he ventured.

Lydia fastened him with a dark look. 'What do you mean, *many*?'

Clearly that information was something he shouldn't be privy to. 'Mr. Hans is most particular about recording these things. He is very thorough.'

Was now the moment to ask about those mysterious addresses he'd seen? 'I wonder – ' he stopped, memory now like fog, amorphous and covering his will. 'Er, I think you should allow him to visit, tell him of your concerns. He's such a kindly gentleman.'

As her visitor was leaving, Lydia gave a base appraisal, if only to bring some normality into the room. He was quite tall, slender and with those bland features, not bad looking – if you liked accountants with a touch of the born again. Put him at thirty-six, absolute max, she calculated, but couldn't imagine him in the sack. 'Got a girlfriend, Ben?'

He ignored that. 'I'm going to report all is well, and you will be expecting another turn.'

'That'd be about right.'

'Goodbye, Mrs. Jellow. Oh, and thank you for the coffee.'

When he'd gone, Lydia slid down onto the floor, wondering what in God's name they'd been talking about.

1919
Twigmere

Second Benjamin and the Widow
That Mezzanine & an Unwelcome Appointment

Benjamin stood outside the hotel in the blazing August sun and gazed proudly across the road to his shop. On the short, if unsteady journey back to the premises, he acknowledged at least a half-dozen patrons and greeted several more admiring the goods on prominent display. Glee & Sons. Purveyors of Fine Beds and Furnishings was a success, a respected establishment in Twigmere's ever-swelling populace. Even the weather seemed to endorse the fact, with a fanfare of summer brilliance, which suffused the place in a golden light.

The proprietor never lacked confidence, or ambition. Since taking over the family business almost ten years ago, he'd replaced his late father's dreary stock and dwindling custom with the best bedroom furnishings of the modern age. Whether it was by dint of his expansive personality or rude good looks, Benjamin seemed to prosper with little more than a nose for fashion. Even during the Great War, which by some miracle he managed to avoid, business flourished.

In other matters, it appeared he was not so fortunate. His wife, like so many, succumbed to the Spanish flu the previous year – a loss he valiantly and swiftly put behind him.

Today it was the widower's fortieth birthday. To

mark the occasion, he'd closed the shop for the afternoon and dined at the local hotel in the company of a delightful friend, also recently bereaved. The lady, a wealthy, long standing customer (and, he fancied, of aristocratic bearing), insisted on paying. After some protest, Benjamin graciously accepted, but on the condition that she received a gift for her young child.

His meeting with the widow, and subsequent friendship, had been instigated in part through a gentleman by the name of Hans, an old retainer of Glee's. It was the very same Mr. Hans whom Benjamin was expecting at his shop this afternoon.

The proprietor's mood deflated, as if a perfunctory hand had reached out and pricked that bloated self-assurance with a timely pin.

He turned the key in the shop door, and stepped within. Gradually adjusting to the gloom, he looked about him: Venetian chests, continental mirrors, French commodes, everything for the discerning customer's boudoir, and all selling well. And beds, of course; they were particularly popular.

He crossed to a private door beneath the mezzanine, the jollying effects of lunch fading.

Upstairs, in the sumptuous sitting room, he drew the curtains and slumped down in an armchair next to the fireplace. Sunlight filtered through the velvet drapes, and reflected in the overmantle. Irritated, Benjamin moved to his bedroom, but even here was unable to settle and returned downstairs to the shop. In this sobering mood, He began to view the luxurious stock with a jaded eye, unwanted memories intruding into his thoughts.

He creaked up the few steps to the mezzanine, and stood for a moment, recalling the advice to his father all those years before. He pictured the rows of brass beds that would be set against the far wall, and felt a longing for the simplicity of those distant times.

It then occurred to him, how the raised floor offered a good view of the street, like a vantage point. Is this why his father had built the floor? 'Pop' Jacob may have been inept, but in those slow thoughts dwelled a sly obstinacy. He hadn't made this just to store those brass contraptions and keep progress away.

Benjamin eyed the banks of dusty ledgers and purchase books. Behind them, boxes held private papers going back sixty years, communications of a dark and peculiar nature. Maybe his father had chosen not to dispose of them in the vain hope that those who came after might find a caution in their disclosure.

The shopkeeper was awoken from his strange musings by an abrupt rapping against the shop window. He glanced down, his pulse quickening. Again, the impatient sound of a cane against the glass.

Tightening his collar, Benjamin descended the steps, and opened the shop door.

An elderly gentleman stood on the threshold, the day behind him setting in an amber sky.

'Good evening, Mr. Glee,' he said, briskly. 'I am here, as per our appointment, to discuss terms.'

He removed a pair of thick, pink-framed glasses and, placing one patent leather shoe after the other, entered the premises. 'Plus the small matter of our agreement in regard to the widow and the care of her infant girl. Shall we commence?'

February 2015
Hertfordshire

When Lydia Asks for Help
&
Escapes with a Temporary Identity

Seven white plastic cups were set on the small table, one for each person in the circle around it.

Lydia stretched out and scooped up the cup nearest her, and took a sip. The water was warm and slightly tangy. From the tap, obviously. She held the cup a little away from her mouth and noticed the woman opposite staring accusingly at her. Lydia glanced up at those present. They were all staring, each with varying degrees of intentness. She placed the cup back on the table.

A middle-aged man leaned forward and slid his hand down the outside leg of his nasty polyester trousers, massaging the calf beneath. 'We do like to begin with an introduction, a brief outline of why you're here,' he explained, apologetically. 'While nothing is taboo, we do expect people to observe cultural and sexual identities and respect the diversities of our group.' He paused, allowing a moment to massage the other leg.

Lydia scoured the room. It was one hundred per cent white Caucasian, with maybe a smattering of dyke in the form of the accusing stare. That bloke was closet. Ex-clergy? Leg molester. Probably why he was here.

'First of all, welcome, er . . . '

'Lydia,' supplied Lydia.

'There you are,' he said, as if half the battle was already won.

Another woman with straight, shiny hair and American teeth flashed a brilliant smile. 'Congratulations on taking the first step, Lydia,' she acknowledged. 'Each week one of us is given time and support to share issues. You'll find we are very honest with each other here.'

'Is there anything you wanna say?' enquired the accusing-stare woman, as if on the hurry-up.

The trouser man, group leader, Lydia assumed, interceded. 'Before we start, it's important to remind everyone that none of us repeat what happens in this room. If we meet outside, we do not approach, unless there is some prior understanding or arrangement to do so.'

Really? Lydia felt the eyes on her again, and for once wasn't too keen on the attention. They were a motley bunch. Couple of blokes and five females, including her. She didn't reckon on this anonymous lark. Let's face it, there was only one well-respected store within a ten-mile radius. There was bound to be somebody out of this lot who perused its aisles. The specimen in the wellies, for instance; he was a prime candidate for the organic section.

She lifted off her Ray-Ban sunglasses and hooked a black plastic arm over the first button of her blouse.

'Do you get migraines?' the accusing stare asked.

'Yes,' Lydia said, and crossed her arms. She'd never considered migraines before and this place was beginning to feel like a bloody headache.

'Well,' she declared, summoning the room, 'I've been having shocking dreams lately. Nightmares, actually, except they're not always at night. Daymares, anytimemares. Even my sofa can't be trusted.'

That didn't raise a flicker.

At this point she felt it necessary to make a clear distinction between her material circumstance and the kind of place she now found herself in. No, she didn't work at the moment, was widowed but now remained happily single, was comfortably off, had a lovely house and everything was fine. It was *just* the nightmares. And possibly the bed. And this man.

'Man?' queried the accusing stare.

Lydia said, 'An old guy came to turn my mattress.' That didn't sound right. 'I'm not into men. Well, I am, in the *normal* sense.' She allowed a symbolic foot to sink gratifyingly into yielding earth.

'Why would you get an old man to turn your mattress?'

'And why wouldn't I? He gets paid the same as anyone else.' Lydia narrowed her eyes. 'I don't know what you sleep on, but it was and is a very expensive bed. And you don't throw away that amount of cash, if you have it, and not expect some kind of after-sales service. Any problems with that?' She slammed her folded arms across her chest, sunglasses clamped in her cleavage.

The welly person spoke. 'You seem very upset by this.'

'Yes, I am, actually,' admitted Lydia, eyes pricking. 'I haven't come here to be attacked. I'm very vulnerable at the moment. These nightmares are ruining my life, literally. I am having a really, really bad time. I think I'm going out of my mind . . . ' She raised her little finger to collect a tear.

Someone said, 'A new bed is quite significant. Perhaps this is really about your late partner.'

Lydia jumped.

They noticed.

'What'd he die of?' demanded the accusing stare.

Did the cow actually say that? Too late. The question, by subliminal group semaphore or sheer tactless brutality, had found its target in Lydia's ever-susceptible brain. The image of her dead husband danced before her. His face was purple and twisted with beseeching. He was begging her to stop whatever she was doing those years before. Leave him in peace and let him stay where he was. He was happy in the house. Why was she forcing him to move? Please, he couldn't take any more estate agents. Stop!

Now a frightened Lydia wished she had stopped and left him in peace, because he wouldn't be here, in her head, tormenting her back. Whichever way she turned, the evidence presented itself. The hideous vision soared like a kite, its strings, she imagined, tethered to her, these people now witnesses to her selfish cruelty.

Lydia squeezed her eyes tight. 'I didn't kill him!'

She heard the gentle pulse of activity, the gluggle of water jugs being refilled, the short gulps as the group, despite its holy ethics, prepared for this thrilling impromptu performance.

A voice began telling her that guilt is very common around death, and asking about an anniversary.

'March,' she squeaked, mechanically. 'Twenty second of March.' A memory skidded behind and caught up, slamming into her brain. Wasn't that the date for the mattress turner's appointment? The room whirled. She said, 'That's when the bastard's coming back.'

'Lydia, we can leave it there.'

But Lydia's eyes were wide and filled with living nightmares. Taunting, invading dreams that needed to be dumped, offloaded, right here and right now. 'I only told him to cash in,' she bleated. 'He was in his seventies. Rattling around in that four-bed pile in Potter's Bar. It was worth a bloody fortune. He'd already had one attack . . . They were all totally past it.'

'They? Who are you talking about? Your partner?'

Lydia was tired. This lot just couldn't keep up. 'What's with the *partners?*' she snapped. '*Husbands!* I married *men* – Retro Hetero that I am. And they're all fucking relics. Husbands, mattress turners. Except him. Didn't marry him.' She fumbled at her blouse and fingered out the Ray-Bans, aiming the warmly scented frames at her face. 'I'll go through it, once. I've had three antiques. One died in situ; two divorced, but even they must be practically dead by now.'

She secured the Ray-Bans on the bridge of her nose. 'And don't ask me about the magician-cum-bed-swinger. That old bastard turned up wearing a pair of ruby-studded specs, like something out of a circus. "Wednesday's glasses," he said. Upstairs, downstairs in me lady's chamber,' she sobbed. 'With my bloody wedding rings.'

'Lydia, these are terrible, terrible dreams. You're not guilty of anything.'

She lolled back her head and stared at the flaking ceiling. 'Yes I am. Even my poor mother didn't get to her coffin un-fleeced. That's what I'm like. This is the thing when your life comes back to bite you in the butt. Extreme Karma!' She struggled to her feet, feeble strings snapping from her arms and shoulders. 'I'm leaving. This is not going to work. He'll come back like Mamma did, to haunt me. I know what his game is.'

'Poor Lydia.' That was the accusing stare.

The nerve.

A stray sentence wafted within earshot. The words 'telephone, vulnerable' pierced the charged air.

In an instant, Lydia had seized her bag and was diving through the mangle of arms to the exit.

No one tried to stop her.

Despite everything, Lydia Jellow was a perfectionist, a fastidious fantasist and tidier of ends. She leaned magnificently against the wall, a heavily ringed hand on a Help the Aged poster. 'Sorry, bit unfair that. I didn't mean it to go so far. I'm undercover. A hack for the local rag. We're checking up on rogue therapy groups in the area.'

No one believed her.

As she made a dignified exit she felt compelled to excise any trailing strands. 'For the record,' she called, 'all my girlfriends are young, gay men.' And she escaped, if not exculpated, into the sane, provincial street.

Making the Call & a Sudden Thing

Lydia caught the train back home, and a safe distance away from theatrics. Touch and go, that.

She'd gathered herself sufficiently, and sashayed up the manicured 'mews' to her front door and unlocked the two Chubbs. Her hand shook as it lifted the Yale key. Perhaps this was a mistake and it was time to think of selling. She leaned the door shut, dropped the keys on a little shelf in the hallway and plonked herself on the bottom step of the stairs.

A grandfather clock, a bona fide if reproduction heirloom, struck seven. Two hours fast. Glee's may still be open.

It was a deliberate dawdle to find the number, knowing a place like that would close at precisely five. Thankfully, when she finally rang, the call went to electronic voice.

'Hi, Ben. Lydia Jellow here.' What excuse could she give? Why should she need one? It was her bed, her life. Her sanity. 'I'm calling about the appointment in March,' she told the machine. 'Haven't been feeling too good lately, and I'm probably going to take a break for a while. Definitely taking a break.'

The phone echoed suddenly and hummed. A click. 'Oh bollocks,' she muttered.

A human voice, although the difference was minimal, spoke. 'Mrs. Jellow, hello. You were saying something about March.'

Lydia rolled her eyes. 'Yes, I'm cancelling. Not feeling great, Ben. I've decided to take a nice long holiday. Plenty of notice.' Her hands were sweaty. She caught sight of her reflection in the mirror; it didn't look like her at all.

'I'm sorry to hear that, Mrs. Jellow. Is there anything I can do?'

'Yes, you can call me Lydia, for a start. Anyway, the twenty second is not possible. At all.'

'One moment, Mrs, er, Lydia. I have a diary just here. I think we may be able to accommodate.'

She could almost hear that accommodating – his limbs stretching and contorting to a diary probably ten feet away, just to make certain.

'Luckily we have a space. When are you thinking of taking your break?'

The crafty sod. No flies on that little bugger. 'Right now, actually, Ben.' She changed tack. 'Listen to me. I'm sick of this. I do not want that man in my house. I do not want my mattress turned or adjusted. I just want to *stop* having nightmares.'

A considerate pause. 'Yes, yes, I can fully appreciate how distressing that must be,' the voice droned on. 'Unfortunately, as I've mentioned, we get terribly booked up. Mr. Hans obviously chose that date for a reason. Can you not hold out?'

'No I bloody cannot!' Lydia bawled. 'I am cancelling . . . Forthwith.' Good that, she thought. Solicitors used it, like 'notwithstanding' and 'without prejudice'.

But like a hand-coiled spring, the voice bounced back. 'I think we need to get this emergency resolved. I'll let Mr. Hans know. Oddly, we have had a couple of these recently . . . '

She hurled the phone to the floor and stamped her

feet so hard the keys bounced on the little shelf. Confronting the hall mirror, she aimed an indignant look, as if communing with it. 'Mamma, I was only young. You've done worse,' she reminded it. 'Okay, I'm sorry. Now tell them to forgive me.'

Tracks of black mascara were riven on ashen skin; even so, the face in the bevelled glass was unexpected. She rocked, blinked and rubbed her eyes. 'Mamma?'

Lurching to the door, she reached for the latch, but changed her mind. Not daring to look again, she bolted to the stairs and scrambled up on all fours to the bedroom, remaining crablike on the floor. It took a while before she raised herself and swayed like a drunk before the mirror.

The Edwardian wardrobe had a good glass that never failed to rebuke. She pressed the switch on a side lamp. In the globe of yellow light, with hands over her eyes, she peeked through the fingers, a glimpse at a time.

Lydia wasn't there. Not the one from the day, the hour before. Revelation or revolution.

Above her tremulous stare sat a nest of big curls, dyed dry blonde from grey. The roots were now ebony black, an inch growth of old, natural colour. A shade she'd not seen for fifteen years. At least.

Her fingers fluttered above the regenerated scalp. Her mind froze on a sentence delivered weeks ago, and then repeated, 'The benefits can take some while, or be quite sudden and happen all at once.'

A dream, but a bloody good one.

She fell onto the bed, ignoring a crinkle of paper, and a small card at her feet. And the rest.

1975
Twigmere

Farewell Second Benjamin, a Funeral
&
When Joseph Sees an Old Friend

The term 'Act of God' is regarded with suspicion by many insurance companies. They hate paying out, especially on 'victims' as old as Benjamin Glee, who should not even be able to walk the streets, let alone hold them to ransom. But when a roof slate loosened by an earlier storm fell from a Twigmere hotel, killing the ninety-seven-year-old, some insisted it was the work of the Almighty's very own hand.

The claim was dismissed and shoddy seventies workmanship blamed, the burden to settle eventually placed on the hotel. For the sake of expediency they came to an arrangement. The only surviving relative, as far as anyone could be sure, was a son, Joseph.

And Joseph liked the hotel, it was useful. No point incurring any unnecessary ill will. His father had to go at some time.

Nonetheless, the incident is worth some comment, if only for its lively nature.

Benjamin had been due to keep an onerous monthly appointment with a Mr. Gifford Hans. Instead he chose to take a lady, a guest of said hotel, out dancing until the early hours. The proprietor was so well fortified that, after returning the lady to her lodgings, he had waltzed back and forth across Twigmere's

High Street. If that was not enough, he had stood beneath the window loudly serenading her, waking the entire street in the process.

And then it happened. A heavy slate from that badly repaired roof slipped, bounced from the guttering and fell, landing with a fatal crash upon his head.

The lady, who'd been witness to the event, was so distraught, (or, on discovering his extreme age, disgusted) she'd instantly returned to London, leaving a sworn statement affirming all she had seen.

Juvenile lapses aside, the late Benjamin Glee had been, to the outside world, at least, the personification of charm and ease.

His quaint shop selling curiosities of a bygone era had also offered a rather staid line in bedding. Yet even in the effete mid-nineteen-seventies, a time of recession and upswept streets, visitors to the Twigmere shop found his talks on the necessity of a good night's sleep surprisingly uplifting. And conversations around this extraordinary little outlet continued far beyond that pleasant town.

Despite his private feelings, Joseph had given a spirited eulogy at the church, and when mourners arrived at the hotel, he had greeted them warmly, with neither rancour nor bitterness on show.

Guests raised their glasses to good old Benjamin, who was at last enjoying his own famous good night.

As the jolly mortician who'd dealt with the body observed, apart from the cosmic intervention, there was not a scratch on him and the old boy could have probably gone on for years. 'Like his grandfather, I understand. Extraordinary longevity, the Glees.'

Joseph listened to the good-natured chatter, relieved

for the sake of ongoing business that his father was held in such esteem.

'Yes,' he assured those who'd asked, 'Glee's would survive even in these straitened times. If not,' he'd acknowledged, modestly, 'with the same verve' as his distinguished father.

As Joseph moved around the room chatting to his guests, he became distracted by a flickering brilliance, a luminous crest breaking on that sea of funereal drear. This radiance, in the shape of a woman, lowered the hood of her long lilac cape and smiled across at him.

It had been over twenty five years since he'd last seen her, and she had not changed a bit. The vivid red hair was loose about her shoulders, those unforgettable grey-blue eyes as commanding as ever, but this time a warning glinted in their widening gaze. She raised a finger and put it to her lips, shook her head and turned away.

By the time Joseph had pulled himself together, Prunella Flaggon was nowhere to be seen.

1859

A Journey Planned
&
Ambrose Confronts a Spectacle

Ambrose eyed the cradle with its slumbering
occupant. His patron was seated opposite and
appeared also to sleep, but you could not be certain of
anything with this one. If the old man travelled also,
could he not deliver his own consignment? And why
the stifling confinements of a coach, when a train
compartment would do? There was something of the
mystery in it all, a too familiar stench. And a penitent
would never lose the nose for that.

He prodded the ball of coins in his pocket and
leaned back in his seat with a thankful prayer. The
journey was in daylight. And still the infant slept.

Tomorrow it would all be over. But what lay ahead
for him then? The day after that? Ambrose was a
sinking man. Regret pursued him in waves, the past
ebbing and flowing, sometimes to a hair's breadth, its
terrors engulfing him once more.

On they rode, and as their carriage swerved and
rocked, Ambrose kept unblinking vigil on the sleeping
man.

The horses were changed, and still no movement
from the cot. Ambrose began to doubt his senses.
Surely, the child would stir by now? This good
fortune had come too easy and a toll must lie in wait.

Purse started awake. He quickly fumbled out the

pince-nez from his cape and was alert in seconds. He leaned over the cot. 'It still sleeps soundly. Excellent.'

'Did you give the nipper a little draught?' enquired Ambrose, nervously. 'My wife used to give the boy a touch of the gin to keep him quiet.'

'I have heard of such practices,' replied the old man, returning the *pince-nez* to his embroidered waistcoat pocket. 'And your wife, did she enjoy the gin?'

'We all like a drop . . . Not too much. Sadly she ain't with us no more,' Ambrose concluded swiftly.

'My condolences. And your boy, has he a taste?'

Ambrose did not answer, his attention drawn to yet another pair of spectacles that his companion was turning over in his hand. Curious, he moved nearer and found the items were fashioned from dull metal into two large, ugly shapes to cover the eyes. But they held no glass and looked more suited to the blind.

'Ingenious,' marvelled the other man. 'You will not have witnessed the like,' and, unfolding the crude arms, he fastened on the spectacles.

They were so clumsy and ill-fitting they covered half his face. It was a fearful sight, and to Ambrose chillingly familiar. Uncertain how to play this mischief, he gave a forced jolt of mirth. 'Oh, very entertaining, sir. Like something out of the pantomime, them. Very good, Mr. Purse. You are right, I ain't contemplated the like before. You are a most resourceful gent, if I may say.'

'And I can see you with absolute clarity.'

'That I cannot believe. They be solid, all one piece. No glazing in 'em, sir. A trick, is it? My boy had jokes like that.'

'Tricks, indeed. And what happened to the boy?'

'Happened?' Fear burned in the scavenger's throat as the objects searched him out, following with their sightless stare. 'Why, the young they make their own way. Can't say I know.'

At last Purse eased off the spectacles and offered them for scrutiny. 'You will note, Mr. Bind, the one tiny aperture. Yet even on the gloomiest day, the weakest eyes will be restored to perfect vision.'

Ambrose received them and passed a coarse finger across the cold metal. There was indeed a small hole, like a pinprick in the sheenless black. 'That ain't enough. It be like a blindfold that would stop out all light. In my mind this be the work of magic, Mr. Purse. I am in God's hands now. I don't keep company with the devil's work.'

'Pray, one try,' insisted the old man, his voice scraping like lead. 'You will discover how the merest glimmer may be the path to greater illumination.'

Ambrose had no choice and, lifting the spectacles, set them on with quivering hands. He sat squeezing his eyes, foolishly waiting in the coffin dark. The metal frame pinched and felt unnatural on his skin, like an insect he wanted to smack away. He became uncomfortably minded of the suffocating air, the crunch of wheels and sweating sickness as the imprisoning carriage pitched across the stony ground.

'Look, Mr. Bind, and see,' urged the old man.

Reluctantly, Ambrose fluttered open his eyelids and stared at the blank spheres. Nothing. Then, gradually, as he concentrated, the minuscule prick of light expanded to a thin tunnel, his scope of vision widening. Suddenly, the rolling daylight beyond streamed into his eyes like glistening rain and he could see.

A portrait framed in black, its subject now more youthful, sat before him. Once fleet and delicate as a dappled butterfly, then ponderous as death itself, the phantom slipped in out and of horrified view.

Ambrose fell back in his seat, his hand at this throat. 'God save me!' he begged. 'You? The devil has come to take me! It is you!'

Tearing the vile contraptions from his face, he was enveloped in a glare of daylight. They had arrived at Twigmere. He was alone in the carriage, the cot on the seat beside him. Pinned to the lace shawl was a small letter addressed to Mr. B. H. Glee. The High Street.

1976
Twigmere

Joseph Makes a List, Something Proven
&
Business Continues

Joseph had his grandfather's soft, ill-defined features. Unlike 'Pop' Jacob, however, there was a parsimonious aspect to his nature, a nose for compensation and a tendency to brood.

The most enduring grudge was toward his late father's romantic indiscretions. Because of this, Joseph refused such dalliances and had remained a bachelor.

Now at thirty-five he'd decided, for the sake of business and the Glee line, it was time to marry.

His fiancée was far from frivolous. An unassuming and sensible woman, she came from an old Hampshire family, who had themselves been in retail.

He didn't know if he was in love with his future wife, or she with him, but the pragmatic heir to Glee's Bedding was satisfied that this sensible arrangement would ensure a life without controversy. And so it almost was.

On this unseasonably hot June afternoon, he'd discarded his jacket and tie and closed shop for the day. Moving to an imposing roll top desk, he set to finalising the wedding guest list. Pen in hand, he began ticking off the names, his thoughts restless. Next to him on the desk lay a copy of his father's will.

Unable to shake off its disturbing contents, Joseph took up the document again and hovered the nib over each line.

He would have been the sole beneficiary were it not for a Miss Prunella Flaggon, bequeathed of a nine hundred and ninety nine year lease on a property in Middlesex. A property that she had occupied for some considerable time.

But why her? As far back as he could remember his father and Prunella had argued.

It was almost a year since the funeral, and although Joseph had been surprised by her brief appearance, he had regarded it as a respectful rather than fond farewell. He'd dismissed that mysterious semaphore on the day as her old nonsense. She'd always been the one for dramatics.

He could still recall her grand entrances at the shop where his father would be reduced to a servile wreck. He might attempt to counter her demands with the odd bark of protest. Yet whatever the reason, Prunella always got what she asked for.

And hadn't Joseph been captivated by the exotic and outrageous creature? Of all the women who'd wafted in and out of his childhood it was 'pretend' Aunt Prunella who defended him against his father. She understood how hurt the young boy had been by those trivial amours, not to mention the slight against the mother he'd never known, whose death (and his survival) was treated with the same careless levity.

That's what he'd thought. Now it all looked very different. Not so mysterious.

He nudged away the document and swivelled round his chair to face the shop floor, a sense of injustice ripening. 'A property in Middlesex, eh?'

Joseph surveyed the shop with a morose eye. Business was slow but steady. These days, people were looking for the more unusual items. Apart from a small display of bedding, the stock was now a mixture of old and new furniture, a trend his father introduced just before his passing. He'd a selection of choice pieces himself, bought in from the good houses and country auctions. In fact, the place was beginning to resemble an antique shop.

Beyond the tall windows, Twigmere bustled in the sun and traffic. A nearby festival threatened days of noise, more invasions of broke hippy types who never brought anything with them but litter.

The fan whispered behind him, the cool air curling his collar. 'Middlesex,' he repeated to himself. 'Near London. How much would that yield over the years?'

He twisted his hand to a desk drawer and slid out a small bundle of letters. He'd found these upstairs in his old room. They were decades old.

Lifting an envelope, he gave an irritated glance at the spidery scrawl, and drew out a single page.

September 22 1949

My Dearest Joseph,
Thank you for your help today. I do believe it was your most gentle administrations that restored my health so quickly and saved me from fainting once more.

Joseph lifted his eyes, but failed to recall the incident.

Aside from the hullabaloo I have some exciting news. Your best pretend Aunt Prunella is going to have a baby. Isn't that wonderful? When she is old enough, (for I am certain of a she), my daughter will visit you at Twigmere.

What a clever boy you are to remember so clearly. I was very impressed by the splendid drawing of him. What a curious thing to happen. So often, you tell me, and each time they are different.

We must keep our correspondence secret from you know who. He can be such a beastly ogre.

Poor, sweet Joseph, what are we to do about it all? I am here to listen when it comes to such things.

Continue your poetry, but do not neglect arithmetic and history. It is most important for your future that you should keep good accounts and remember your kings and queens.

I do so look forward to any new intrigue, and enclose requisite funds for comics, pencils, paper and other distractions (and comforts).

With lots of fond wishes
Pretend Aunt Prunella

His fingers beaded through the letters, skimming their content, all written in the same flowery language.

He came to a loose page with a few lines dashed across. Turning it over, he checked the date: July 12th 1954. Just before his fourteenth birthday. Did they correspond that late?

The handwriting was still as poor, but the writer was no longer speaking to a child.

P.S. I have just received your letter. Thank you for alerting me. And you've witnessed this first hand? How alarming.

I've found him to be most persistent. He will appear when you are least expecting and least resistant. The Glee family were, by their original actions, always terribly susceptible. My own had their weakness, too.

This has become a rather sad last letter to my favourite pretend nephew. Remember what I said about keeping your accounts in order. The future is never far away, the past is even nearer. Adieu

'What actions?' Joseph shook his head. Drivel and silly riddles. If she'd distrusted his father and the Glees so much, then why the hell should she benefit from them?

All this sentimental reverie no longer held sway. The past had been a ruse. Something rotten in it. There was no friendship between him and Prunella; that had long since been betrayed. Pretend is what she was and that nonsense had no part in his life now.

Stretching from his chair, he glanced up at the clock. It was already ten past five; the heat had put him in a daze.

He buttoned his shirt, grabbed a tie and left the shop for an appointment. Business is business, even on half-day closing. Especially if there's a wedding to pay for.

February 2016
Twickenham

Sophie's Rediscovered Place

Where was Sophie? Even Sophie wasn't sure anymore. Her eyes were bleary and limbs leaden from lack of sleep, days passing with the weight of juggernauts.

She slung a cardigan on over her pyjamas and plodded barefoot down the hallway to the door.

Reaching for the latch, she wondered if there was any point in opening it.

The 'hardly ever here' upstairs neighbour was back. She leaned against Sophie's side of the small porch, one hand carrying shopping, the other on the wall's blistering paintwork. She said, 'You look like death warmed-up, love. Can I come in or do you want to go back to sleep for a couple of years?'

'What?'

'Hello, Sophie!' the woman almost shouted in that 'make a bloody effort' voice. 'Popped in to see if you're okay. Would've come earlier but been on the telephone all morning having issues with the roof in France,' she said, her tone shifting to, 'We all have problems, mate.'

Sophie said, 'Hello. D'you wanna come in?' and slunk away.

'How about we go in here for a change,' called the neighbour, pointing to the front room. 'I don't fancy wading through that lot. And I've bought some sandwiches for you . . . Sophie?'

Sophie was sliding down the wall, her mouth bubbling. Tears flowing, dribbling down her neck and plopping onto her hands.

'Oh, Christ. Sorry. Sorry, love. Come here. What is it?' The neighbour, her shopping spilling on the floor, gave an ungainly embrace, all elbows and awkward knees.

Sophie's convulsing misery fell into what effectively was a stranger's arms, and she couldn't speak for several minutes.

The neighbour helped her up and guided her into the front room, cold and damp, and sat her on a velvet couch. She tried to light the gas fire, but had to find her lighter first. 'Come on. What's the matter, love?'

Sophie focussed on a mirror above the brick fireplace and steered her blurred gaze around the naked room. One sofa, no carpet and bare, splintery boards. She never, ever came in here and, forgetting her visitor, rolled back her head and gave a long groan.

'Listen, Sophie, you're depressed. Sometimes a short course of tablets can really do the trick. Something about the chemistry in your brain. We can make an appointment with the GP, if you like.'

'I told her that she was a lonely old cow. No, not cow.'

'Who, love? You talking about Prune? Is this about your granny?'

'I said Mum hated her.'

'I reckon she'd probably worked that one out herself, love. I wouldn't worry about it.' The neighbour slid a cigarette from her bag. 'Don't mind, do you?' She clicked open her lighter.

Sophie didn't, except when the smell wisped across her face. 'She's all burned now.'

The neighbour funnelled smoke from the corner of her mouth. 'To be honest, I hadn't realised you were that close. She was very difficult. It sounds to me as if you've got a bit of grieving to do. It's all mixed up with other stuff around your mum. I shouldn't say it, but she didn't have an easy life with her. No one did around Prune. Amazing in loads of ways, but not what you'd really want as, you know, the primary emotional provider.'

Sophie turned away and coiled up, resting her cheek on the tall back of the couch. The fabric smelled musty and reassuringly decadent. She felt a hand at her back. The contact was warm and genuine. This is what a touch feels like. 'I don't know what I'm going to do now,' she whimpered.

'Nothing. You don't have to do anything.'

'The old man came around to turn the mattress,' Sophie sniffed, still not moving. 'I have bad dreams in that bed. You called it a sarcophagus.'

'Oh, for God's sake, Sophie. It was a joke. My big mouth. Get rid of it if you don't like it. Get rid of everything. Is that what it is, you feel buried alive in here?'

'No. I just wish she was sleeping in it again.'

'She was ninety eight, love. Believe me, she lived and slept long enough. You didn't do anything wrong. Prune was many things, but she didn't give a flying whatsit what anyone thought of her. She loved you, in her way, and your mum. And you've got this now.' The neighbour shrugged her shoulders in the general direction of crumbling plaster. 'You're very lucky, really.' She tapped Sophie's shoulder. 'Have you spoken to her, your mum?'

Sophie shook her head.

'I think you should. Probably been through the mill herself, you know.' Back in the hallway, the neighbour sorted out the bags and returned with a selection of sandwiches. 'Tuck in. By the way, I've decided to rent out upstairs. Won't be for a month or so until I get a new boiler.' She peeled out a limp triangle of bread. 'Hey, that's an option for here, when you get sorted. Letting it out.'

Sophie swung around to deliver a firm 'No,' then settled back to her position, and picked at a baguette.

The neighbour wrinkled her brow, eyes narrowing on a nagging detail. 'What was that about the mattress and old men?'

'Man,' Sophie mumbled. 'He's supposed to be coming back. This other guy came round to check up to see if it was okay. I've taken over Granny's contract thing.'

The neighbour's face curved around and met her dead stare. 'Contract thing? For that bed?' She sat back. ' Be careful, love. No wonder you're having bloody nightmares.'

'He'll stop them. That's what it says. The mattress needs adjusting. 'Sophie bolted upright, her utterance like a gust of air, dusting the room's melancholic corners. 'I think I'll be okay now. And I could do this up, couldn't I?' She saw the frown in her visitor's eyes, a look that doubted she was capable of anything.

'That's the spirit.' The neighbour turned her head quickly to snatch that edge of the something threatening to slip away. 'Sophie,' she said, tentatively. 'This mattress guy? When's he coming?'

'It's on a card they sent. Don't know where it is.'

'Well, let me know. If I'm around, I'll come and meet this mattress man and his contracts.'

Sophie tried to imagine what it would be like if someone else were present, sharing the experience, whatever that would be. Even with the merest memory of the old man she'd come to feel stubbornly possessive of him. She regarded the neighbour, who'd never shown interest in her before, with sly calculation. She was an interferer come to ruin that exclusive attentiveness, which had brought two strange men to her door. 'It's ages away. I'll be okay.'

If the hurried-out neighbour was amazed at Sophie's swift recovery it was tempered with relief. Despite her genuine concern for the young woman, she was probably thinking that the last thing she wanted now was more drama downstairs.

Promise Made

Sophie waited all afternoon on the window seat in the damp front room.

She knew when Mr. Hans would arrive. The card he'd sent that week was hidden in a drawer. The surprise appointment had been made 'earlier than was usual', due to an emergency.

Emergency? Whatever misty vagueness hung around that Christmas Eve, she was certain of one thing: the mattress turner's age. He was very old.

So was he ill? Dead?

Maybe it wasn't even him who was coming to do whatever needed doing to the mattress. This idea seemed to crush her spirits further.

'That Ben better not try to send anyone else round,' she whispered bitterly. Anyway, she wouldn't let them in. It must be Mr. Hans or the mattress would stay unadjusted, and she'd never sleep properly again.

She pressed her cheek against the cold window, breath quick and white on the glass. More of those easy tears tickled the corners of her mouth.

Upstairs was quiet, the neighbour safely not there. Still Sophie's thoughts wavered from one helpless outcome to the next.

Leaving her seat, eyes still fixed on the window and view of the front path, she stepped to the gas fire, the back of her legs to the low flame.

She wore a clean skirt, an ironed silky top and a pair of proper shoes. She'd washed and dried her hair and combed it until it shone. The mattress had been stripped, bedroom cleaned, but there wasn't a lot she could do with the living room, so she had carried the much admired Ernest Gimson chair in here, for her visitor.

How the distinctive Mr. Hans walked down the road, into the garden and up to the front door without her seeing, Sophie had no idea. Yet here he was in the front room and sitting quite comfortably on the spindly chair, she opposite on the long couch, his presence quenching the silence with thankfulness.

The fireplace had a brick surround with little steps down to the hearth, like cantilevered niches. Two cups rested untouched on either side.

Sophie had pulled the heavy curtain to, because the light was in her eyes. There was no bulb on the ceiling rose and Mr. Hans now sat in semi-darkness, his rimless glasses almost invisible against parchment-pale skin.

He wore a pair of beautifully polished brogues and a maroon and green tweed coat overcoat with a cream buttonhole. She couldn't make out the flower properly but thought it might be a lily.

He rested one hand on the silver top of his walking stick, removed his trilby with the other and placed the hat on his knees, the brim pincered between thumb and forefinger.

As if to complement the action, she folded her own hands on that Sunday best lap, and said, 'Is everything all right?'

He nodded and slipped off his glasses, snapping them grasshopper quick into a pocket.

She noticed how bright and clear his eyes were, even in the gloom. 'I don't know what to do now.'

'Indeed,' he said, mysteriously, and inclined his head. 'Are you rested?'

'No. Not really.' Sophie stood as if in preparation for something and smoothed down her skirt.

The curtains were dusty and the walls by the ceiling stained with tea-like-brown rings. 'Sorry it's such a mess. I have tidied the bed. I can't actually remember.'

She caught sight of her reflection in the mirror above the fireplace. Her face was pale and a little thinner than she'd expected, a new, soft curve brushing beneath the cheekbones.

When Mr. Hans returned to the front room, he bowed briefly and reached out. The cuffs of his pink silk shirt were studded with amethysts and on a finger of his left hand a wide wedding band glinted like a golden promise.

Without prompt, Sophie offered the small fee. She had remembered that.

'It is a mere token, of course. All is adjusted. Everything is turned. We will not meet again,' he said.

At the mirror she stood on tiptoe and drew her finger over her naked lip, then angled her head slightly to find a different view. Gathering a handful of hair, she twisted it and piled it in an untidy chignon on top. As she dropped her hand, a defiant smile bloomed in glistening eyes, and fine strands of hair cascaded like broken sunlight at her neck, a flare of red in its shimmer.

'It's not so bad,' she said to her reflection. 'Not so bad. I'll manage. I always do.'

2015
Surrey

A Sad Visit, Being Benjamin
&
A Possible Change of Direction

Glees had their family grave in a churchyard just outside Hindhead. On this late February day, Ben stood before his father's headstone and experienced a perverse sense of renewal. There was a lush evergreen and hopeful air about the moment, as if spring had just arrived.

'I'm off to see Mother now,' he informed the grave. 'I expect you know anyway.' Leaving the gentle enclosures of conifers and moss, he continued briskly onto the nursing home where his mother now lived.

It puzzled him how he always recognised her. His mother was a shrunken line, a dot on a chair, amongst all the other dots, on other chairs in the modified grandeur of the sitting room. Yet he knew her shape, in a way an abandoned item of clothing is identifiable, because the imprint, the memory of its wearer is somehow left inside.

She greeted him, distracted, and gave a flutter of her hanky to the nursing staff. Perhaps they could bring her guest tea, or coffee, for goodness' sake, after his long journey.

The conversation between mother and son would be limited and without sequence, but her random chatter could reveal more than she would, in perfect health, have allowed.

'Has he been nosing around again, dear?' she murmured.

This was becoming more frequent. 'How are you, Ma?'

'I'm all right, but I think your father should show more authority. Tell him to go away. That man is driving him barmy. Now we've had to put up in this hotel.'

Ben squeezed her hand. 'Who are you talking about?'

'You should know. My husband's being tormented by him. He's terrified. I think this is much more serious than we first thought.'

The lightness of earlier vanished.

'How's the shop, Ben?' Her return was equally disconcerting and tantalisingly beyond grasp. 'Must be hard going these days,' she said. 'Your father had the same problem, especially after he became ill. And he wasn't as organised as you.'

A nurse brought a tray of tea and biscuits over and set it beside them.

'Thanks,' Ben said. 'Here we are, Ma. Shall I pour?'

But she was off again, about glasses and purple breeches, the devil incarnate and calling Ben, Joseph, and telling him that he was far too weak.

He pressed a goodbye kiss on her cheek as she slumbered on her chair, in a place he would not have been able to afford without his father's prudent foresight.

The nurse saw him to the door. 'Everything all right, Mr. Glee?'

'Is she getting worse?'

'Like everyone, she has good and bad days.'

'I think I'll have a word with the manager next time.' Ben looked across the lawns to the tall hedges, and drew some comfort from its calm regularity. 'She's only been like this recently. Seems distressed, fixed on an idea.'

'It's difficult not to try and make sense of these things, I know. She loves seeing you, that's the most important thing now.'

'Thanks. Thank you.'

'See you next time, Mr. Glee.'

The long driveway was like an avenue of trees leading from a country estate. Ben never got used to reaching the end and the shock of traffic that greeted him.

Turning left, he made his way through Hindhead, up to the common and the Devil's Punchbowl. He found a bench and sat, gazing across the steep hollow, sifting through his mother's words.

There was both sense and no sense, he thought. A catch of reason amongst her unspooling mind, a thread that may connect to something. Had his father really been unwell before his accident? No. If anything, he'd had a new lease of life. Everyone expected him to be another long-living Glee. And then he had the fall, and seemed to give up the fight and diminish before everyone's eyes.

And not all the Glees endured. Great-grandpa Jacob also passed relatively young.

So is it just us lucky, robust Benjamins destined to go on and on? pondered Ben, wryly. 'What a prospect,' he said out loud.

It began to rain. Beyond the fine drizzle, distant

pathways fell like ribbons from ragged escarpments; a spine of purple trees nudged the sky. Ben glanced down at his fingers turned white in a sudden chill.

This latest witness to his mother's frailty jarred against unlikely tales of his enduring namesakes. She would soon be lost to his world and the shared past that filled it. Was he prepared for that? He was just another shopkeeper, another Glee carrying on the family business, which, with its layers of obstinate dead, was beginning to resemble a graveyard itself.

Below him, mist skated over lakes of bracken; above, a fret of birds swooped in the tangled air.

He hunched up his coat and dug his hands into the pockets. Winter had returned and Ben was tired. Tired of business, telephone calls, hysterical clients and follow-up appointments. Who said Glees should exist doing the same thing forever? He got to his feet and wearily followed the path down to the car park and its little café.

A pink rose of sun hung in the afternoon sky. Sharply alert, as if just waking, he saw his own path. It had once seemed that this road was as predictable as heavenly sunsets were to the rotation of the earth. But if he refused to be that kind of Benjamin Glee, if he dared deviate, would he fall? Possibly. He knew nothing else.

He laughed quietly to himself. The result of his tumbling would not be a giant cauldron like the one hollowed out in Hindhead. It would be the shallowest imprint of a nobody on ancient Surrey soil. A landing as imperceptible as dust settling on an old abandoned ledger. He was content with that.

1910
Twigmere

First Benjamin – the Final View

After all the years of what he'd regarded as services to bedding, Benjamin Horace Glee felt no nearer to rest. His poor wife was long gone and his own life unfurled before him like an endless, inexhaustible road, mocking his endurance at every waking day.

How old was he now? A hundred? More. And they'd had electric lights in the next town for almost thirty years.

Benjamin stood ramrod straight in his sitting room above the shop. With his pale folds of craggy skin and harsh demeanour, he was still a peculiarly commanding figure. His thick hair was snow white, those brooding eyes hooded by a heavy brow, the mouth, with its once cruel sneer, now concealed by a moustache.

Removing a rosewood pipe from his waistcoat, he knocked the bowl against the marble fireplace, and tipped the loosened ash to the fire. The powder floated slowly to the flame, a grey breath, a memory reluctant to be dismissed.

He felt in his jacket pocket. Remembering he had left his tobacco downstairs, he placed the pipe on the mantel.

He moved to the window and inspected the street below. Jacob was there, pacing in front of the shop, nodding to passers-by. 'Nodding won't pay the bills, you dullard,' muttered Benjamin. 'You ain't a dog performing tricks to please the beggars.'

It would be that young Benjamin who'd save the business. He often heard the boy talking loudly to his father, putting him right, no doubt. The grandson was sharp as mustard, he mused, and a good-looking boy. Plenty of get-ahead. Queer that.

Benjamin Horace turned, crossed to a cupboard and lifted out a box. It felt very heavy today, as if its contents had gained weight since the last time. He carried it over to a table and carefully removed a ledger and placed it on the polished wood, lifting the cover. November twenty eight, eighteen fifty nine, the first entry stated. The writing on it as bold and clear as if the ink, like blood, were still drying. Benjamin shuddered at the memory. It could have happened last week it was so vivid in his mind.

The letter was there, too, folded between the first and second pages. But its message was almost gone, rubbed out with age and, apart from the words, '*gift of hands,*' the writer's testimonial unclear.

'It *is* just the one?' Hans had asked of Benjamin's misdemeanours, fifty years before. As if the old fox hadn't known his every sin. And in turn for his salvation? Jacob. A soft plodder, who'd rather play with trains than run a business. He had no more gumption about it now than a dunce at school. This is what that devil had called hope.

But they'd kept their word and brought Jacob up as if he were their own. And, as promised in return, none of them had wanted for anything that money could buy.

Yet even Benjamin had to admit a certain

attachment. Whatever cures and curses he'd agreed to, they did not belong with the bastard sons of strangers.

He glanced down at the letter, and traced a finger over the fold marks, the loops and curves of now diminished script. He looked over at the fire raging in its hearth, and back to the window; the taste of soot was on his tongue, and he spat on his hand.

Beyond, the sun was beginning to lighten the winter sky, naked trees reaching for an amnesty.

And below? There he was, Gifford Hans, rounding the corner, spectacles perched on the end of his nose. He raised his bowler hat to the window in a taunting salute.

'No!' cried Benjamin. His hand reached to his chest. 'Leave the fool be!' The pain shot down his arm and pierced his ribs. He banged at the glass, shouting a warning to his son. As he watched the mattress turner creep closer, he felt his heart shatter in his breast.

But Jacob had not seen Gifford Hans's approach. He'd heard the banging at the window, looked up and witnessed his father's stricken face, and rushed to his aid.

In the sitting room, the old shopkeeper called a name, perhaps in prayer. He staggered toward the fireplace, crushing the letter in his hand as he fell.

When Jacob arrived at his father's side, it was too late. He uncurled the fist, placed his own hand on the sleeping face to make sure, and then called for Minnie.

Jacob sat, feeling neither sorrow nor judgment, and waited for his wife.

2015

Going Backwards & Lydia's Trip

Mrs. Jellow had never learned to drive. If she had, she would have certainly jumped in her motor, probably a classy retro MG, and roared full throttle down to Twigmere. Once there, she would have had words with Ben Glee and demanded the address of Twigmere's finest mattress turner. And then?

Lydia hadn't got that far with the scene. Suffice it to say, once she'd found Mr. G. Hans, she would most likely fall to her knees and beg the old bastard to marry her before she was too young for it to be legal.

In truth, her age reversal was not that dramatic. More a gentle backward roll, like an old Rover with the brake loosened, creeping down a Surrey hill. Anything could halt its trajectory. Another car, for instance, or house. You can never tell what you may hit when going back end first.

Mrs. Jellow wasn't in the mood to anticipate disaster – she was sitting facing the direction of travel on a train conveying her to that enchanting Surrey town.

Arriving at Twigmere's station, she grabbed a free paper to check up on the local property prices.

She was demurely dressed in a smart late 1950-style suit with the jacket pinched at a newly wrought waist. Clutching a discreet matching leather handbag, she tottered on three-inch heels along the pavement toward the High Street.

The pavement was perilously narrow, and she was

forced to pause every now and then to allow lorries to pass for fear of being dragged beneath their wheels. That would be ironic.

Safely in the town centre, she found a decent café and ordered a light lunch, and sat pondering her approach to Ben Glee.

He was probably the sort to get huffy when a phone was thrown down on him. That repressed type could never handle emotions, theirs or anyone else's. Best carry on as if nothing had happened. After all, this was an emergency. What concentrated her mind (and body) now was the cause of this remarkable change. To guarantee it lasted, so to speak, it was important to find out who or what was responsible. The bed or the mattress turner? Merely the results of 'restorative sleep', to quote the men in taupe coats, could not repair a decade or so of well-used life?

Sipping at her cappuccino, Lydia scanned the café's stripped floorboards, its heritage-coloured walls and the trusted openness of the counter bulging with cakes. Lulled by the ambient murmur, she heard its blissful cadence scattering mention of that well-respected store. Twigmere was hers by rights.

Beyond the sparkling window, she could see the war memorial. She remembered sitting freezing there on that little bench, and the old bloke with his silver stick parking himself next to her. The room tilted slightly. A silver-topped stick?

Lydia scrambled in her bag and pulled out a purse. Waving a tenner at the girl, she then slipped the note beneath her cup. She left the café without even a memento, her freshly waxed legs buckling beneath her.

2010

Joseph Makes Late Enquiries & Starts Again

'I sat here with your father over half a century ago. It was the day I moved into *his,* at that time, auction cast-off,' Prunella said, digging a fork into a slice of dry beef. 'I did promise this place would serve better food. Alas, dear Joseph, that moment also passed you by.'

Swamped in a vast angora jacket, feather boa fluttering at her neck, she brushed back a wisp of pale red hair. 'I see you are of the other lot and look your age.'

He offered up a hesitant smile in response. Joseph Glee was fit and healthy but, lacking Benjamin's luxuriant raven locks, his hair was scant and skin appropriately weathered by sixty-odd years. Yet etched in those flaccid features was a familiar, harrowed expression.

'The maisonette was a good investment,' she said, watching him carefully.

'My father had a knack for picking winners. I'll give him that,' he acknowledged, quietly.

'And you haven't? What did I tell you about keeping accounts?'

The proprietorial Joseph glanced around the pub to see if anyone was looking. The diners seemed indifferent to the eccentric dress and shrill, imperious tones of his aged companion. In fact, nobody gave her a second glance.

He took a mouthful of steak pie and watched Prunella pick at her lunch, setting the vegetables to one side. It was amazing she still had her own teeth – he shifted his view for a sly interrogation. Yes, they looked real enough.

He reckoned the creature must be in her nineties if she was a day, but in that long flowing skirt and languishing like a modern Isadora Duncan in her chair, she could be fifty. 'What about your daughter? I never heard any more about her.'

'Neither did I. She moved out as soon as she could and went to live with her father. A wise decision on her part.'

'So you divorced?'

'I never married.'

Joseph said, 'Oh.'

'I've always regarded marriage as a form of subjugation, if not the prostitution it once was,' Prunella told him with enthusiasm. 'Now, of course, it has become a murky fiscal compromise with all the self-deceit that incurs.'

He had no idea what any of that meant, but was tempted to ask of her murky fiscal compromises in regard to his father's estate, but didn't. It was a long time since Joseph had been that straightforward.

'My daughter is damaged, I'm certain,' she continued, matter-of-fact. 'Mostly by the lack of domestic convention. Normality is very punishing.'

Joseph lowered his fork and wondered if he'd been wise to drive up here and take a batty old woman out to lunch. Except she was worse than mad, completely immoral. 'Is, er, he still alive?'

'No. I'm blamed for that, too.' She flicked at her

boa. 'More to your point, Joseph, is why I am still breathing. This is what you're wondering, isn't it?'

That threw him. 'No, no. I'm delighted you look so well. Marvellous, for your age. A miracle,' he said, picking up his cutlery again.

'Let's talk about you now,' she said.

He gave a self-conscious cough. 'Well I've been very fortunate, I suppose. My wife has been a wonderful companion, she's . . .' Pausing, he made a swift if odious comparison with his wife's age and the mystifying creature before him. It just did not seem fair. 'She stopped working in the shop a while back, but I won't retire yet.'

'Glees never retire. Offspring?'

'Yes, we almost gave up, and then our Ben came along. He's a good, steady, lad.'

'Another Benjamin. Surprised. But why break the habit of lifetimes?'

'Yes, seems to be a family favourite, but it was my wife who chose it.'

Prunella stretched up and looked around. He couldn't decide if she'd no appetite or was bored, and reached for his wallet.

'I know them,' she said, to his embarrassment or shame-faced relief. 'It's settled. I couldn't allow my pretend nephew in his distressed state to pay. I am not a monster, you know.'

They left the pub and strolled down a tree-lined street to a park. It was a well-tended area, with all the signs of middle-class complacency and he could not resist that masochistic reckoning of how much his father had given away.

Prunella touched his arm. 'Would you like to see the

apartment? I'm assuming that's why you're here.'

Would this be a Flaggon too far? 'I really wouldn't want to impose. If you're sure, Prunella. But I won't stay long. Traffic gets bad after four.'

They turned left into another road, this one without trees, and walked back in the direction of the main road. She stopped at a plain terrace of maisonettes. The downstairs one had a square bay, with a few tubs of flowers outside, the garden gate off its hinges. It was, compared to all the other properties in the road, conspicuously, if not provocatively, the worse for wear. 'Here we, or rather, I am,' she said, and threw him an impish smile 'You'll be relieved to see how awful it is. Follow me.'

The hallway was damp and there was no evidence of central heating. He removed his cap and placed it on the hallstand.

Prunella kicked off her pumps and willowed down the corridor, passing each door with a cursory flick of her hand. At the end of the hall, she announced, 'middle, dining or sitting room,' and gave what looked to Joseph like a twirl. Still theatre-mad, he thought.

And it was like a stage set. Or sale room. Early English chests, a campaign trunk, sofas and what seemed like endless chairs were crammed into the space. Walls were smothered in photographs, prints of dancers, programmes and framed Variety posters. A pair of ballet shoes floated from a wrought-iron lamp.

'Very interesting,' he said.

'I knew it would be too much for you.' She directed him back down the hall, and disappeared to make refreshments.

The front room was cool and relatively spartan. Joseph seated himself on a long moth-eaten couch and noticed the damp in the corner: guttering. He better tell her; that would only get worse.

She brought in a tray, elbowing his help away, and set it down on a small Chinese table. 'Sit. I'll be pretend mother; I have enough practice.' She poured the tea and then arranged herself on the window seat, her legs crossed, cup in hand. 'I do remember those marvellous drawings and letters you used to send me, Joseph. I think I still have a few hereabouts.'

He had no memory of such things and looked around for the sugar.

'Would you like some brandy instead?' She abandoned her cup and scampered off again, returning with the drinks. She handed him a glass and knelt on the couch with her own. 'What is the matter, Joseph? You've always been such a disgruntled soul.'

He didn't know what to say and took a sip of brandy; fire in his throat.

The front door slammed and someone crashed into the hallway, the thud of footsteps, their clumsy tread lumping to another room.

Prunella held her glass to her ear as if it could help her anticipate the direction of travel.

Nothing for a moment. The footsteps returned and stopped outside the door with a palpable silence.

Prunella threw back her head. 'Sophie,' she called to the ceiling. 'Would you like to come in?'

A young, unsteady voice, said, 'No, Granny. I'm in a rush.' A rustle and the front door slammed again.

'My granddaughter is more gauche than rude, Joseph. Not her fault.'

He gave a nod and assumed the girl was yet another casualty from a messy life. 'I best be off, Prunella,' he muttered, rising to his feet. 'I don't want to be in the way.'

She patted the seat. 'You're not. Sit down, we have a lot to discuss. After all, why make this long journey to just tootle off?'

It doesn't take much to invoke the past. The mere register of voice can trigger memories consigned to emotional ditches decades back. In this case, it was her steely look that put him in his place. Now he couldn't find the words to explain how he'd felt those years before.

'Is this to do with Benjamin?' she said.

Joseph's legs ached and he creaked back onto the couch. 'I suppose, I wanted to fathom exactly what your relationship was with my father,' he said, taking a full slug of brandy. 'You didn't seem to like each other very much, as far as I recall.'

'But you remember us,' she said. 'You and I were friends, united against the common enemy.'

'Yes, and then I saw you at the "enemy's" funeral.'

'Over thirty years ago. And this is the soonest you could arrive here to bring your grievances?' Her voice was flint hard, cold eyes covering him with disappointment. 'This gift to me must have come as a surprise,' she said and poked him in the arm.

He flinched and scuffed his shoes on the bare floorboards. 'You two were always at loggerheads. It didn't make sense.'

'He gave a promise.'

'Who to?'

'To whom. I can't say, Joseph.'

He swilled brandy around the glass and then raised it to his lips, words muffled. 'Sounds more like something else.'

'I can assure you, it was business. Old, tiresome business. And it didn't start with you.'

'What about your mother?'

She rested a firm hand on his arm. 'What binds us is not always blood – in your case it appears to be a matter of nurture over nature – and money certainly divides.'

This sounded like rambling to Joseph.

'And here you are,' she reminded him crisply, 'at an inopportune moment in your business. So, I must ask, what is it you want from me?'

'Nothing.' He felt a familiar churn of regret and caught her eye.

Apart from the cobweb weave across the face, she still had that same mischievous look. The mouth wide, high, the face sharp with those high cheekbones. But the hand he saw on his arm was withered like an autumn leaf, its tissue like flesh shrinking from the veins. Hadn't his aged father's own supple youth also been betrayed? But for him it had been the anguished looks, a craving for rest.

'I suppose I was a bit rattled,' he said, artifice now beyond his reach. 'And you're right about business, it's rock bottom,' he admitted, keen to move the talk on. 'We've been at this a long time. I don't want to hand over the shop to the boy in this state. I'm waiting for things to pick up.'

'There are other options.' she said, her tone easing.

'I won't bow out. You know that.' Joseph relaxed, a renewed trust leavening his tone. 'Anyway, we're into beds again and considering new stock. A completely different range. Top end, stand out quality this time. Twigmere's not London, I know, but it has plenty of old money. I'm pretty confident we have a chance, especially when we get the advertising sorted. The boy's good at that.' He heard his words straying from their usual steady flow, and chuckled. Setting his brandy down on the table, he said, 'I do believe you've made me tipsy, Prunella.'

She sat motionless beside him.

'Interesting really. The agent worked for us, years ago. What you'd call a real gentleman. Quite severe and very, very persuasive. We're not fixed quite yet; these beds are phenomenally pricey.'

Prunella let him continue as a parent would allow an excited child to spill the day's activities.

'Because of the special materials sourced and the workmanship, some of the mattresses run into tens of thousands.' He laughed, almost incredulous, as if confronting the absurdity for the first time. 'Cashmere and silk, would you believe? I only hope our Ben develops a silver tongue, because he'll need it. The thing is.' Here he frowned, doubt catching up. 'They've got a deal of weight to 'em. Truly great, hefty things. I couldn't lift one.'

Prunella's presence flickered at the rim of his vision. Her scrutiny like a weight itself seemed to be dragging him away from this one last chance.

'I don't have a choice,' he insisted, pre-empting any challenge she may offer. 'This is an excellent product. And I just have the capital at the moment. I am not going to let Glee's go down the pan after, what, a hundred and fifty years?'

She didn't respond.

He'd been talking far too much. A part of him, that young pretend nephew, perhaps, sought reassurance. 'I am doing the right thing. It's a huge investment, at my age. I'm thinking of our boy, really.'

'Naturally,' she said, at last.

'There will be a follow-up supplemental service to the beds, of course.'

'As night follows day.'

'We'll offer a reconditioning package. Have to call it something more than that. Give it a label, catchy phrase.'

'You will.'

'Mattress turning sounds a little basic.'

'If that's what it is.'

He didn't seem to hear. 'The exclusive angle needs to be marketed alongside the beds. Bespoke, sort of thing. Customers do like that. I think this character can pull it off.' Joseph had shuffled into the hallway, still a little heady from the brandy. 'Funny old boy. Needs a bit of getting used to. I'm confident that he can manage.'

'He'll find a way.'

'My father certainly did well with him. I said I'd give him a year, see how the land lies after that.'

'I wonder how long he'll give you.'

His hand was on the latch and he tugged at the door.

'It sticks. Give it a good yank, Joseph.' She folded her arms and leaned against the wall, her face angled towards him. It was a fragile face. Human, nothing like the spectral vision of last time, or even of an hour before.

'Sometimes, Prunella, I wonder what spirit burns in

you and not in us mortals.'

'Well, don't. You can barely manage brandy.'

He laughed at that. 'By the way, I really can't remember drawings, or letters. Next time, eh?' He took up his cap, folding the satin lining in and out. 'Do you know, I've got photographs of all the Glees outside the shop? Going right back to the eighteen hundreds, when my great-grandpa Benjamin took it over again. You can see the resemblance in my father.'

'How remarkable.'

'Glees had a lot of property in Twigmere in those days.'

Outside, the world was tamed, ductile and light. 'I don't know what I expected today. But I've got to admit, it did put the wind up me. After what we'd gone through years back and then finding someone outside the family had an interest. I got to apologise for that. I should have sorted it out before this.'

'Grudges have been nursed for longer, Joseph.'

Smiling, he took her hand. 'Well, I'm glad we met again,' he said and kissed her lightly on the cheek. 'One for old time's sake. All forgiven, pretend Aunt Prunella?'

Closing the gate, he felt her watching, and remembered he'd said nothing about the guttering.

1966
Twickenham

A Momentary Contrivance

A length of lace hangs at a bedroom window. Apart from when the magnolia is in flower, there is not much to see.

The window faces south. A tall fence stands to the right and a brick wall on the left casts a perpetual shadow; as a result, the bedroom is always dark and cool, even in summer.

A cheval mirror is pushed to the corner next to the wardrobe. A few dresses are scattered on a large, ornate bed. The only light in the room is from the weak glow of a small electric lamp.

In the garden, the magnolia tree sleeps, its branches cold.

If someone were to stand outside today, between bathroom and fence, and peer beyond the patterned veil into the room, they would find a female of indeterminate age. She stands regarding herself in the long, silvered mirror.

If the viewer creeps back along the wall, they'll come to another window, this one curtain-less. Within this unlit room, a slim, pretty girl in her teens kneels, rocking back and forth. She begins to shout into the air; the words are indistinct, muffled. She jumps up and rushes from view.

Darting back to the first window, the observer will witness its occupant move quickly to the door, and then jump back, startled. The young girl rushes into the blurred frame and, raising both hands, shoves the woman to the floor.

At this point, the prying someone may want to intervene, but can't.

The woman recovers and rises to her feet. Except for her trembling, she remains perfectly still. In that rigid stance, she appears more threatening than her assailant, who now backs down and begins to cry.

Although the woman attempts to console the girl, she pushes her away and leaves the room.

Most would find witnessing a domestic quarrel uncomfortable, but this interloper remains at their vigil, waiting for another scene to unfold in this story.

The woman is alone and stares ahead, her arms empty.

The viewer crouches down beneath the window sill, back to the wall, and faces the garden. To the right, a narrow border of earth meets the fence. They become aware of neighbours' comings and goings beyond, of gates being opened, a squeak of a bicycle being wheeled down an alley. The front door slamming.

They return their attention to the window.

The timber on the bottom stile is rotten and doesn't meet the apron properly, allowing a gust of wind to enter. Because the catch is also loose, the frame shudders and the lace moves a half an inch.

In the intervening unwatched seconds, the woman has dressed in a long silken gown. Her face is painted chalk white, her hair coiled into an elaborate knot. She sits at the window, absorbed in writing.

The viewer can see the delicate lines of distress on her furrowed brow, the tightening of her mouth. As she bends her head, tiny stars like jewels blink among the flame-red curls.

She reaches up and bangs at the window frame, clicking the catch back and forth. She moves away and the watcher gradually draws themselves up, senses trained.

They hear the short, shrill blast of a doorbell. The borrowed glow from the window is gone as the lamp is switched off.

The room is still and void of colour and life.

A male figure now enters the scene, followed by the woman. The man is elderly and solemnly dressed.

The woman approaches the bed and points to it. She hesitates, glances toward the window, crosses to the door and vanishes from the picture.

In a jagged lightning instant, she has reappeared, climbs onto the mattress and lies down. Her face is buried in its covers as if deep in slumber.

The man looks on for a moment. Removing his hat and long, black coat, he begins to undress. At this point, the viewer may want to look away, but is unable to avert their eyes, and waits for the spectacle to be over.

Through that captured picture window space, a small candle now burns on a table, illuminating the vast antique bed. An intricately carved headboard looms over the burgundy satin coverlet, where the woman lies. Shadows ripple along the wall, lengthening and shrinking, the old man cupped in darkness.

Stirring, the woman raises herself and reaches out.

Across the bed, two naked, youthful bodies entwine. Light and supple, radiant in the glowing dark, they flow together among the satin waves, the candle flame dancing at each delighted breath.

As quick as a shutter lens, all is as it was. An old-fashioned gentleman bows graciously, while the woman stands over a desk and reaches for her purse.

The observer's gaze will float invisibly to the window and, like smoke from a gutted candle, slides beneath to breathe again.

March 2015

All Good Things & Bad

The shop faced onto the wide, busy High Street. Its large window was lit and the display of fine beds visible for all to admire.

Lydia peered through into the back of the shop and saw the indistinct shape of steps to a raised floor, and what looked like a large desk. She couldn't remember any of that from last time.

There was no movement or sign of life at the premises. Her gaze searched the door and the window for opening times, but there was only her reflection in the vacant glass. The shop was closed. Typical: when you want them, there's nobody about.

It felt like a rebuff. A child dressed up to go to a party only to be told that it's the wrong day. A bright, best show-off entrance, a singular moment of triumph that cannot be reprised.

Lydia didn't think in these terms. An infantile petulance, a ball of windy hurt swelled beneath her ribcage and forced a tiny expulsion. 'For fuck's *sake*.' It was an incongruent accessory to her 1950s ensemble.

She drew a hanky from the clutch bag and dabbed at her nose. She needed to find that Mr. Hans. The only thing to do now was to try pot luck in the town. If the old sod was prone to the afternoon constitutional, he'd be bound to collapse onto a bench, eventually.

It was cold, the sun weak in a cloudy sky. She

sniffed again, and braced herself for the long haul.

'Mrs. Jellow?'

The relief at seeing the dullest man that ever lived was almost poignant. Like souls once cleaved apart though the misunderstanding, now ushered together in an expedient reunion. A well of exhilaration brimmed in Lydia's grateful heart.

His coat politely flapping and tie discreetly loosened, Ben Glee ambled toward her as correct and understated as Twigmere itself. She was surprised to see that his hair had lost its corrugated look and was actually windswept.

Another involuntary quiver on those eyelids, a winsome smile puckering in blushing cheeks. He was not bad at all; shame he'd been born too late.

'Hi, Ben. Thought I'd pop in to see you. Shame our conversation got cut off last time. The phone went completely dead. They were digging up the road outside. You know what these cable moguls are like, chomping into everything. They do say we're never more than ten feet from a rat.'

Ben was staring at her, his brow drawn into a knot of disbelief. 'Mrs. Jellow?' he said again.

'That's me, Ben. Yes. See what you've done?' Her hand gave a sweeping gesture as if she were shedding a giant cobweb, or her skin. 'Well, your mattress man, Mr. Hans. I think he's responsible for the new me,' she teased.

Ben summoned a feeble smile. 'You did say you'd been unwell. You seem to have recovered.'

'Oh, God, yes. Fully, fully recovered, rejuvenated and resuscitated. I don't think even a year's supply of ginseng could have done me more good.'

He was at the shop door, key in the lock. 'We are actually closed for the afternoon, Mrs. Jellow, but as you've travelled some distance, perhaps you'd like to come in.'

Gone was the starchiness; even his back seemed less rod like.

'That's really sweet, Ben. Slightly impromptu this. And there is something I need to ask you.' She followed him into the shop.

The interior was different: smaller, bigger, taller, lower. What was it? The smell. That was it, a musty, old smell, and damp, when somewhere has been locked and left.

The strip lighting buzzed on. It was very harsh and made her skin look jaundiced. She flâneured across to a divan and sank onto its plastic protector, rotating her arms across the expanse of mattress like a broken windmill.

Meanwhile, Ben had seated himself at the roll-top desk. 'Excuse me a moment, Mrs. Jellow.' He opened a letter, instantly absorbed in its contents.

After a minute or so she began to fidget. 'Well, anyway, if you can give me his address, I can pop around and arrange the next appointment. Save you the bother.'

'Sorry, Mrs. Jellow?'

'Lydia.'

He cast a harried glance in her direction. A jolt, and he was in automaton mode. 'We need to make another appointment.'

'That's what I've been saying. Not necessary. I'll go and see him myself, you know. I'd like to thank him, personally.'

'Who?' Ben swept from his seat, hurrying to a set of stairs leading to the raised floor. 'Just a moment.'

She watched him climb and pace across the creaking floor, and then crouch behind the banister-style railings, looking for something. He straightened up and leaned over, a filing box in his hand. 'I have an awful lot to do,' he told her, and with a few long strides he was down the stairs and back at his desk.

'Is this because of the phone?' she asked, more in panic than contrition. 'I do get a bit over the top when I'm stressed.'

'Nothing to do with you, Mrs. Jellow. We do have other customers. If you can just bear with me, I will answer your query, I need to check a date. It's important.'

'Go ahead, I've got all day.' Lydia lay back and stared at the ceiling's ornate coving. She remembered lying just like this on that first visit to Twigmere. What a difference a year makes, and this bed was nowhere near as good as hers.

'I'm considering moving, Ben,' she informed his preoccupied silence. 'The prices here are very reasonable, and I've got a good vibe about this place, you know.' She rolled over, and prodded the mattress, her nails digging into it plastic covering, and then her eye caught the door beneath the mezzanine.

'Do you live above the shop?' Lydia curved around, flung her legs in the air and gave her shoes the once-over. 'You do get a lot of accommodation above a shop. But then you have the worry about change of use. Who wants curried curtains, or undertakers shunting stiffs about all hours of the night and day? Not what I'd fancy. Still, don't suppose it matters in your case. Leasehold, is it?'

She bounced up from the bed, and began slinking about the floor, running a hand across a headboard, squeezing a pillow. The clock said quarter past three, but surprisingly it was already getting dark outside. Wandering back towards Ben, she said, 'I better go, if you're busy . . . So, can you give me Mr. Hans's address?'

He looked up, panic streaking across those even features. The phone was ringing. Then, as if in slow motion, he turned from her and lifted the receiver.

She stamped her foot, temper rising. 'Come on. I mean, he's not bloody royalty. You don't *own* him.'

Lydia regretted that. Even she sometimes invested concern in someone else and, judging from his expression, things had just gone south in the Ben Glee department.

The whole of him was grey, shrunk like a plastic bag, sucked hollow with the shopping thrown out if it. He dropped the phone awkwardly, the receiver slipping from the cradle.

Lydia walked over and clicked it into place. 'Not a good time, eh?'

His eyes were blank, their focus broken. 'It was the nursing home,' he said quietly. 'My mother. Gone. I was only there – '

What could Lydia say about that? 'Sorry. Sorry, Ben.'

Ben nodded toward the door, words distant, defeated. 'He lives up the hill, by the railings. I can't remember the number now. Old cottages, timber. You'll know when you see it. He won't be in. I can tell you now, because I'm not long back myself.'

Lydia crept away before the visceral scent of a stranger's grief reached her nostrils, the toxic particulates of someone else's pain stuck in her throat.

Outside, the bossy clicking of her heels echoed along the narrow curving pavements. 'Up the hill, by the railings,' she repeated. Whatever propelled her, or whatever she was propelled to, it was more important than anything else.

On the other side of the eerily subdued road, there was a row of shops, to the right, a sweep of iron railings fringing the start of a small hill. She darted across and made her way to who knows where exactly. But she'd know it when she saw it, Ben had said.

Ahead, the roofs of old cottages blushed beneath the cool kisses of a winter sun. To her left, a screen of trees, the sound of their branches like the rustle of a taffeta silk dress as it sways with each balletic movement of its wearer. This place was magic, out of this world. If this is where Mr. Gifford Hans lived, she could settle here forever. Never move again.

A flash, or glitter, of something bright by her side, was replaced by a fleeting steel-like coldness. She shivered; someone must've stepped on her grave.

On Lydia walked, searching for the old man, who would surely bring her everything a woman like her deserved. The sharp clip of her steps sounded up and down that ancient Twigmere hill. On and on like the endless ticking of an everlasting clock.

2012

A Visitor & Joseph Remembers

Arms folded, chin deep in his chest, Joseph eyed the figure in the corner of the room. His mind bobbed like a little boat over the memories of Benjamin, and pictures of his old great-grandfather surged up in waves. When he came to Prunella his thoughts seemed to stall, unwilling to move on. He just could not find what it was that bothered him. 'I still can't believe I walked the Seven Sisters.'

' Highly commendable, Mr. Glee. And back?'

'And back. A good ten miles. I could not have done that thirty years ago, if ever, Mr. Hans.'

'A feat indeed. Quite remarkable.'

'I feel younger than I did than when I got married. My wife – ' Joseph broke off, his thoughts darkening. 'She worries, thinks I'm on steroids.'

'How is your wife?'

Joseph refused to be drawn into any more idle pleasantries. There was business to discuss.

The mattress turner pre-empted the change of tone. 'Your son has ambitions for the shop?'

'Now we're doing better, thanks to you, I think he could make a go of it.' The shopkeeper paced over to the window, his fingers plucking at the net curtain. He could hear the bell tinkle downstairs, voices raised in greeting and young Ben's flat tones. 'He worked at one of the big stores for the experience, got to manager. Wants to get stuck in here. Running your own business is very different from being on the pay roll.'

'Quite so. Very different.'

'But we think he's ready.' Joseph swallowed, his mouth dry and thoughts reeling. Why did this old rogue give him the heebie-jeebies? Sitting there every month. Worse than belonging to the bloody masons; the Jehovah's Witnesses could learn a lesson or two from him. He certainly had the staying power, and now, oddly enough, so did he. It wasn't natural. Yes, that's what it was, endurance. Why did he feel twenty years younger, when his poor wife was all aches and pains and losing her memory? His father had been the same, dancing and gadding about.

He peered across the road. The hotel was having a wedding reception, he could tell, by the girls falling out, in all respects, onto the pavement with their little posies, men swaying about in top hats and tails. Imagine that, he could see it all quite clearly without his glasses.

Last night he'd dreamt of Prunella. She was wearing a long gown and prancing around like a ballerina, letters showering over her like leaves from a tree. Was the old fiend still alive? This Hans certainly seemed to be going strong.

All the while he leaned at the window, studying his thoughts, the old man sat studying him. Joseph could feel it. He said, 'I can't guarantee that he'll want to keep you on, Mr. Hans. I can't promise that, I'm afraid.'

The replying silence had a shape, like one left in a seat, an old leather seat that the incumbent has occupied for some time. An imprint of silence.

Joseph tried a shrug, insouciant, and tidied the curtain, lifting it up, shaking it down. 'For a start, how am I going to explain the accounts to him? My Ben is very particular about accounts. He doesn't like any straying or lackadaisical oversights. Everything must be in its place. There's a name for it. He's like that. Rigid.'

'What are you suggesting?' queried the voice in the corner, disturbing that imprint.

'Well, I do not think that we can carry on,' Joseph said, meting out the words as if they were his last. 'If I retire, as I intend to do, I cannot automatically pass you on to my son. And he will be running the show; effectively he will be boss. I will have nothing further to do with the business.'

The figure of Mr. Hans rose and emerged from the shadow until he came into clear view. Producing a pair of old-fashioned *pince-nez* from a pocket, he balanced them on his withered, angular face. 'This is most unfortunate. Agreements are not entered into lightly.'

Joseph's heart was beating hard, his stomach ice cold. How could this happen? What power did this creature have? 'But it was my *agreement,* as you put it, Mr. Hans. It did not include my son. He's starting out and entitled to make his own arrangements.'

'You forget. Quite understandable, for it was some time ago. Of course, it has little to do with your son, notwithstanding his relationship to a business I have supported for many a long year.'

'I'm sure we have expressed appreciation for this, for many a long year, but the matter still stands. Benjamin will be his own person.'

'As you are your own person? As each of the Glees before you have been their own person?'

'I don't understand.'

'Perhaps you should take a seat, Mr. Glee.'

Slumping on a chair next to the dining table, Joseph searched out the wood's bevelled edge, his fingers clammy with sweat.

Why? Was he being held to ransom, a ruddy secret code he'd inadvertently broken? His father probably signed up to something and now he was left to pick up the tab. Well, why should he?

The old man seated himself on a chair opposite. 'You don't recall our little conversations all those years ago?' he teased, holding his walking stick upright.

'Afraid I don't,' Joseph said and glanced up. 'What do you mean?' He held the image of the bespectacled man in his gaze for a few moments. The antique glasses reminded him of something, or someone. He lowered his eyes, endeavouring to locate the memory.

A visceral dredging of senses, a subtle conjuring of the past, like a smell brings back the colour of wallpaper in a childhood room. In the same way that Prunella had invoked the boy he'd been, simply by looking at him, this merciless devil, who crouched before him was now teasing out all those buried things.

An intense sapphire blue fired behind the man's small oval lenses.

The shopkeeper lurched forwards, his own eyes searching that implacable face. 'You mean . . . But it's impossible. That was over half a century ago.'

The old man placed his walking stick between his

knees, allowing it to rock from side to side, like a metronome.

'I was a wretched child. A boy.' Joseph's voice was the strangled beseeching of a man, whose own bitter whining has come to deafen him.

Drawings. Letters. Hadn't Prunella mentioned letters? 'I'm not that person anymore.'

'Quite so, Mr. Glee. When we finally awake, we wish it were all over. I can only lift so much at my age.'

It was impossible to reason with the past, Joseph realised. All the other Glees hadn't meant it, either. He had woken, as they undoubtedly had woken. He wished in his very heart that it was over.

1955
Twigmere

A Short Discordant Note

A tin box containing letters lies open on Joseph's bed; coloured pencils and paper are strewn across the counterpane. The boy sits cross-legged among the chaos and writes in an exercise book, his back to the wall.

Occasionally, he'll abandon the writing, bounce up to the casement window and peer at the street below, looking for someone, and then tip back onto the mattress.

The shop door slams below, its bell tinkling wildly. He hears a roar and then the sound of his father as he thunders up the stairs. Joseph rolls over, quickly hides the box beneath the bed and crumples a sheet of paper into his pocket.

Another door slams, his father curses, and then all is quiet.

The boy is back at the window and pressing against its glass. There he is. The old man turns, catches his gaze, and holds it like a hand may clasp another, reluctant to let go. Funny, uncomfortable.

Those two must have had a meeting, Joseph decides. Something always happens to his father when he meets the old man.

On the bed, Joseph bends over and dangles his arms, groping beneath the dusty iron base. He pulls out the box again, removes the letters, rolls onto his stomach and begins to study the pages. He looks up, his eyes narrowing, defiance and wilfulness hardening in his face. Shoving the letters beneath the bed, he tiptoes to the door and cautiously twists the handle.

On the stairs, he holds his breath over the creaks of floorboards and his telltale journey down. He weaves through the shop's warm darkness, around the blind shapes of beds and furniture, fumbles at a tall desk, pulls out a drawer and collects a key. At the shop door, he reaches up and grips the bell's tongue. He unlocks the door, closing it quietly behind him and slips outside into the evening air.

The old man has disappeared and Joseph stands in the quiet street. A few cars are parked along the road, including his father's, but no one is about. The sign on the hotel is beginning to flicker alight. He wonders if this spying was a good idea.

He dawdles along the road until he comes to some railings. Almost forgetting, he kicks at a pebble and dribbles it along. His foot finds another and he lifts it with the side of his boot. Good shot, over the railings. He hears it fall with a satisfying crack, and wanders on.

Ahead of him, a figure moves slowly to the familiar tap-tapping of a stick. At first, the boy holds back, but then imagines he and the old man are characters in an adventure, and creeps silently behind him and up the hill.

The gentleman spins around, a move the boy does not anticipate. They face each other.

The old man smiles, his eyes as blue as the first glimpse of summer sea. He gives a little nod.

Joseph remembers what to say. 'I'm Joseph Glee.

You work for my father. I seen you hanging about the shop loads of times.' His eyes fix on the man's shoes. 'I just wondered what you do for him.'

'We meet at last, Master Glee. So your curiosity brings you here.'

Joseph quickly looks around. 'Is this where you live?''

The man doesn't answer.

'Are you the Mr. Hans he talks about?'

'For your purposes, I am him.' The man bows. 'How can I be of assistance?'

The boy shrugs, his courage faltering. 'Nothing.' He kicks at the kerb. 'You can help me, if you want,' he says awkwardly, 'like you help him.'

Mr. Hans, who had bent slightly to address the boy, straightens and surveys him with cool appraisal. 'By *him*, you refer to Mr. Benjamin Glee?'

'I heard him say it's down to you the shop takes in the money. Well, it'll be my turn one day.'

'I see. You require assurance in this matter?' As though he were calling the boy to attention, the old man raps the cobbled street with his stick. 'Before one enters into any form of contract or agreement, one first should show both circumspection and a willingness to trust,' he warns, censoriously. 'A difficult combination, it must be acknowledged.'

Joseph, who hasn't really listened to that, says, 'I wrote it down here, in case you forget, being so old.' He tugs out the crumpled note and offers it to the man.

'So a wish to secure a legacy before it is too late.' The man twinkles a smile, and plucks the note from the boy. 'Follow me.'

They walk up the hill together and arrive at a row of

small cottages. Mr. Hans motions to a bench next to the railings. 'Let us sit.'

Joseph watches him remove a pair of tortoiseshell-framed glasses from his waistcoat pocket.

'They're always different. How many of them have you got, Mr. Hans?'

'If you are talking of spectacles, and if it is any of your concern, as many as I require,' he says and he begins to read the note.

The boy leans nearer, disheartened by the reproving tut-tutting of his new companion.

The man lowers the page and removes his glasses. 'I find that eyewear is very affecting. It offers variety for a stranger's view of one, and one's view of strangers. It never fails to entertain.'

'What did you think of it, sir?' asks the boy, keen to keep his attention on the letter.

He leans back and peruses Joseph, a gleam in those bright blue eyes. 'You are impatient to know, of course.'

On go the glasses again, and he holds the page aloft, a good distance from his face, and rolls his head from side to side, hand clasped to his chest.

It reminds Joseph of his English teacher's exaggerated way of reading poetry. Mr. Hans, it seems, is laughing at his efforts.

Suddenly the old man frowns. 'There is much to be considered here, and you are to be commended for your powers of observation. The lines are composed from the heart. Are you certain of what you say? You are on the brink of manhood. Time is merciless. When a deed is done, its influence stretches far beyond mere innocence.'

'But you can help me?'

'Can a man serve two masters? Your father and I already have an arrangement.'

'But why should he have everything? He's always cussing you,' Joseph says too quickly. 'I wouldn't cuss you.'

'An agreement should be suited to both parties, it is true. Perhaps you are right.'

The old man rises from his seat, his back straight and standing much taller now. 'You miss a mother, naturally,' he acknowledges. 'This is quite understandable. Yet we cannot act on the assumption that all injustice or misfortune is to be recompensed. I, too, was driven in search of such adjustments. I wonder over the many years, whether its prosecution has not been a little too severe, and perhaps indiscriminate.' The old man raises his stick, parrying at the boy, who remains transfixed. 'I will return with my thoughts on your matter in due course, Master Glee. In the meantime, have I your agreement in preparation?'

Joseph digs his hands in his pockets, shoulders heavy with a bewildering sense of burden. 'What for?'

'Our partnership, when the time arrives?'

'Now?'

'This is what you came for? Your letter expresses a discontent and envy in your relations with your father, and you wish to claim from him what you imagine has been taken from you. For one so young, such preoccupations are burdensome. As you have already noted, Master Glee, I am old. A man of my years can only lift so much without willing participation.'

The boy is nervous and nods. He takes the cold,

outstretched hand. What is a handshake to someone he doesn't know, or of something he doesn't understand? But a feeling of shame makes him shiver as he rushes his goodbye and runs back home.

At nearly fifteen, Joseph Glee has confessed his worst secrets to a stranger and invested its bitterness in him. A young man should know better than to dishonour his own father.

Arriving back at the shop, he's greeted by the sound dance music and good-natured laughter coming from the upstairs sitting room.

Joseph tries to quell the feeling of treachery, but it rises into his throat and hurts his head.

He remembers the letters earlier and his dismissal of the warning. But when he calls to mind the recent conversation, a face does not appear. The old man's image is gone, events evaporated. Joseph has forgotten everything.

Then, caught in a moment of simple joy, he bounds up the stairs. In his room, he turns on the transistor radio as loud as it will go, as any lad his age would do.

Autumn 2014
Twickenham

Falling Once More & Almost a Centenarian

Prunella selected the chiffon gown and dressed. After tightly crossing the satin ribbons of her ballet shoes, she straightened in front of the long mirror. She was a relic. The pearl-white skin like a gossamer veil drawn across ancient bones, the boundless life within, a ludicrous entrapment. A spirit at war against the enduring frame. It had gone on too long.

Gathering her faded hair, she twisted the feathery strands on top of her head and then clipped on a headdress of gauze feathers. 'That won't last,' she admitted.

Her hand played at the window's broken catch. Beyond the glass, the magnolia still bloomed, tipping a blush to the mirthless sky.

She shook her head, and sighed at the prospect. 'I doubt they'll have the gumption to see. People do like to chew on the gristle, get their teeth stuck into a grievance. Mind you, we can talk, gnawing on old wounds for God knows how long. But you always said have faith. How many times have I believed that, my love?'

She absorbed the image of the room, its full wardrobe, overwhelmed desk and the years of settled grime that clung to the smothered walls.

She reached out to the bed and touched the coverlet, feeling the cool satin beneath her fingertips, drawing her hand across bolsters and cushions. Climbing onto the mattress, she curved into a pillow, pressing her face in its lavender fragrance. The linen was always as new, spotlessly clean. A necklace of watery beads glistened on the pristine sham.

Rising, she swung effortlessly from the tall bed, and stretched. 'The park today. An arabesque, perhaps? They pretend not to notice, far too urbane to be affected. It is the modern paucity of spirit.'

She curtseyed to the window and, sweeping along the hallway, left her flat without locking the door.

A few afternoon strollers and dog walkers flecked the village green. A glimmer of sunshine pierced the thinning clouds, the sky behind promising to be as blue as the fondest gaze. Prunella approached that stage of autumn leaves as it rolled out before her and felt the familiar cacophony of nerves. She took a long, deep breath, stood *en-pointe* and then, wisping to the middle of the park, began.

He was there, the old devil. A swagger, dapper in his burgundy velvet frockcoat and black silk top hat. How did she look? Too much powder? Too little rouge? Her hair was not as it should be, and that headdress loosening with every move. What can he expect?

Playful, twirling his cane, he tried a few steps himself. Not his forte, stick to melodrama. She laughed, and pirouetted after him as he darted across the iron bridge. 'Why do you do it?' she called. 'You're too old for play. We are gone on too long.'

He gave a deep and elaborate bow, flourishing his hat.

'Now do stop and listen to me. Am I a monster? Tell me, honestly, Mr. Purse. What have I done all these years? Am I really this ghastly creature they talk about?' She'd returned to the park now, near the magnificent copper beech, her ribs aching. He was behind her, an arm at her waist.

'You don't answer me, so I know it's true. I am always so despicable, and they do hate me. I leave a heritage trail of chaos and misery behind. And yet that has never been my intention.' She caught her breath, pain searing across her breast. 'Has that been our intention?'

'I, too, begin to see the error of it,' he said.

She halted at his waiting hand. 'Don't. I can't, Humphrey. Not now. I'm too tired with shame to dance.'

'Then allow me to assist.' Her partner, invisible to the unconscious world, threw down his cane. His hands cupping her slender waist, he raised her to the heavens.

Descending from her *grande jeté,* Prunella saw the earth fall beneath her. She drifted, caught in one hand, then the other. 'I was almost a centenarian, you know, Mr. Purse. Next time, perhaps.'

'That's the spirit, my beloved Mrs. Purse.'

March 2015

Bravo, Sophie

Sophie was becoming used to answering her door to people she didn't really know. Even today and at eight-thirty in the morning, she was already awake and dressed.

It was the Putney antiques dealer, who'd attended the gathering and sat on the spindly chair, ringing the doorbell at the ungodly hour. She'd been up since four at a trade fair. Avarice, like insomnia, never sleeps.

She'd popped by on the way home. Just to say hello. Oh, and about their little talk, to see if Sophie had thought any more about the unwanted pieces. And, of course to find out if she was feeling better.

Perhaps from her point of view, a decent interval had been allowed. A calculation of three to six months between event and action was perfectly respectable. Any longer, you'd lost the call.

Sophie wasn't privy to the wily machinations of dealers, but something about this woman put her on edge.

She was jittering impatiently on the front step. A clump of hair had strayed from a plastic clasp and hung limply over one eye.

When Sophie let her in, the woman slithered down the hallway, her nose palpating with that sixth sense, (or seventh) and, finding her prize, stood wobbling in the bedroom. 'Jesus Christ,' she'd uttered, weakly. 'I heard about the bed, but the old witch never let me see it. How did I miss it last time? Was this room locked when I was here? You must have locked it.'

Apart from being miffed by the reference, Sophie didn't know what the woman, old witch herself, was talking about.

'Never seen one in the flesh, as it were.' A milky caterpillar of sweat gathered on the dealer's bleached moustache. 'You do know what you've got here, don't you, Sophie? We're talking museum quality. Not that I'll be able to shift it for ages, which means a fortune in storage costs,' she pointed out. 'This will be an overseas buyer, probably Japanese. They will die for this. Heart attack time. I'll take some shots.' Her eyes seemed to project from her skull, and dart like a viper's tongue around the room. Next, she was up the corridor and in the living room, gasping in spasms of unbridled assumption. 'The Gimson. That chair I sat on, remember?'

'I put it in the front room,' Sophie said, and panicked. 'You can't have that. I'm not giving you that. You can have other stuff, like the settees.'

The dealer's face twisted in pain. 'Settees? The bed and the chair are what I'm interested in, Sophie. The bed, primarily. It's the bed I want. The damp has got to most of the other stuff. I can take the campaign chest off your hands, but the desk in the bedroom is a bad marriage.' She gave a condescending toss of her head. 'It's been buggered up by a late addition; the top's wrong.' Folding her arms, the woman continued itemising the previous owner's transgression: 'watermarks on the Mackintosh *style* students' bureau, the bookcase is repro, your textiles have been eaten and the rugs are so filthy I really would not handle them. The flatware, I *might* be interested in, but the bottom is out of the market on that, and I'll have to have a good look. The prints, not sure. Now I'll take some shots.'

'No. You can't.'

'What?'

'I'm going out. I've got to go out.' Sophie said, unsure of the firmness of her ground. 'I'm not selling them to anyone else,' she added, hurriedly.

'I hope not.' The woman's face registered a fleeting hurt, her pride wounded by someone she'd believed to be too stupid to distrust. She stalked down the hall, her mouth set in a gash of fury. 'Waste of my time really.'

'Why? Did I ask you to come?'

The dealer pulled herself together. 'Well, call – Have you still got my number, the one I gave you?' She broke off. 'What *is* that. Whose is *that*?' She pointed to Mr. Hans's small burgundy card with its white lettering. 'What does it say? Let me see.' A predatory claw reached out. '*Mattress turner*?'

If a shadow could make a sound, Sophie heard it crash between her and the woman. She said, 'Nothing's for sale. You've got to go, else I'll miss my train.'

Twigmere
Brave Men & True
or
Change is as Good as a Rest

In his shop, Ben sagged by his desk, raw and grieving and ill-prepared for customers, least of all this one. Directing his eyes toward the tinkling bell, he dismally contemplated the figure, unsure if he'd missed an appointment.

A muddle, slightly reduced in bulk, perhaps, presented itself in the cautious opening of the door, carrying a plastic bag.

'Ben? This is Glee's? I didn't know if I had the right shop. I'm Sophie,' she said. 'Don't know if you remember me.'

He nodded. 'I'm sorry. I should have been in touch.' Rising from his seat, his legs felt weak. 'I've been closed for a few days. Had to make sudden arrangements. Takes a while to deal with these things. We're still not fully open.' He tripped on the chair leg and wobbled.

'Are you okay?' Sophie asked and edged toward the desk.

She wore a decent coat and the hair was brushed and looked more ginger than he remembered. With a little weight off her face, which looked as if it had actually been washed, she was almost presentable.

'I'm fine. Thank you.' He sat again.

'What arrangements?'

'Personal. Sorry. My mother . . . ' His mind seemed to stretch and wander. 'Had to deal with a few things.'

'Your mother? Oh.' Sophie's left eye twitched. 'You mean she's … Is she . . .?'

He coughed. 'Yes, it was . . . It's a few days ago now.'

'My granny died.'

'I remember you saying. She was ninety-eight,' he said wearily, also recalling the last time and humiliation she'd served up on the doorstep.

Sophie said, 'I still can't get rid of her ashes, and I don't even know if I liked her. It must be even worse for you.'

Ben nodded, his energy sinking. This needed to be cut short.

She dithered as if unsure whether to stay or go. Hovering there, clinging, to what? Not a welcome.

His gaze fell away from her and across the shop floor to the ranks of beds, like serried rows of graves. He tried standing again, this time his feet firmly on the ground. 'How can I help?'

Sophie's eyes sparked with purpose. The face tilted towards him was disarming, and the words uttered had childlike candour, inasmuch they trumped the need for tact. 'I came because I don't need you. I want to cancel everything,' she said.

This was becoming a habit, Ben thought. And a relief. Hadn't the Jellow woman stalked off into the sunset? 'Rather a long way to come? You could've telephoned.'

'Been cut off. Forgot to pay the bill. Back on again next week. I mean, I can pay it, just forgot.'

Ben looked away.

'I'm getting myself together, though,' she told him, as if he should know. 'Got to now. Probably have the place done up. Someone came round to have a look at the furniture. Most of it's rotten, apparently. I think they just say that.' She gave a long sigh. 'You're really tidy, I'm not.'

Her rambling was so ingenuous and uncontrived that he found a mindless comfort from it.

'I haven't actually been this far out for ages. You forget when you're stuck inside. You can get totally stuck, actually,' she assured him, moving to the beds and reading each label. 'I almost missed the stop. Wow. These are expensive. Is that for everything?' She pressed the mattress's polythene cover. 'Very different from mine.' A note of pride lifted her voice. She crooked her neck for a better view of the base, and wrinkled her nose. 'Mine's all wood. A proper bed. Antique, actually. It is very big, but I won't sell it. Not yet. And I am sleeping better,' she offered, in case he needed reassuring.

Ben wondered how long she intended fluffing about. 'Glad to hear it. Well, thank you for dropping by and letting me know. If there's nothing more.'

She bit her bottom lip, eyes searching the room. 'Can I take some of these leaflets? For the future.'

Ben nodded. 'Yes, please take a brochure.'

'Actually, there was something. Do I owe you anything?'

In that instant, the notion that this hapless woman could owe anything to anyone appeared ridiculous. It was she who had the deficit; life had clearly short-changed her. Despite her intrusion, he felt very mean.

'No, of course not.' He turned to the desk and lifted that month's catalogue, a dense, matt black affair with glossy pictures. 'Here take this. Something to read on the way home.'

He followed her to the door. As he pulled it open, she grabbed the catalogue. Her other hand caught the door at an awkward angle, and knocked her plastic carrier bag, its contents spewing to the ground. 'Oh, bugger.' She bumped to her knees, scrabbling at coins, grubby paper, and broken lipstick cases on the concrete. A familiar burgundy card was stuck to a packet of tissues, along with a return railway ticket.

'Let me help. You'll need this.' As Ben bent to pick up the train ticket, he saw her bottom lip quiver.

'I'm a mess,' she hiccupped. 'I try not to be, but I am.'

His instinct was to recoil, but instead he kneeled beside her on the step.

'Thanks,' she sniffed. 'You've changed a bit. Not that I actually know you.'

≈≈

After Sophie had dawdled off, all her possessions restored, Ben shut shop. Another one bites the dust, he thought.

When did Glee's last take on a new client, or the delivery of a bespoke bed? Gone, it seemed, were the days when customers rang, frantic for appointments, when, every week, letters were sent with new addresses to Mr. Gifford Hans. There used to be so many clients to deal with, follow-up appointments up and down the land.

Bolting the shop door, he turned the sign, still ruminating on recent events. This time he'd made no effort to persuade Sophie to continue. Just as well; he had found no sign of her in the diary. She was one less dysfunctional client to deal with.

Things really were winding down. Business had dried up. Unlike his father, however, he would be making no effort to revive it. Why bother, if his reward would also be an untimely end?

Ben sank onto a bed and gazed up at the ceiling's ornate coving; that could do with a lick of paint. He could see the tawdry glint of brass frames propped in the corner. Whatever possessed him to order those in?

He lifted his eyes to the mezzanine floor.

The family's history was all up there. Apart from a short period, Glee's had been in the Twigmere's business directory for almost two hundred years. From aged tyrant, philandering entrepreneur to his own father, their handwritten ledgers now yellowed in the dust.

Of all of the Glees, Ben thought, 'Pop' Jacob sounded the best. With his passion for the railways and tales of those famous visits to the Isle of Wight with his beloved Minnie, he was the most human. The odd postcard and memento from Osborne House could still be found upstairs.

And now, after all this time, Ben was going to stop it right here. Sell. Glee's would cease trading.

The room felt unusually quiet. He was overwhelmed with weariness, and dropped forwards, head in his hands. His eyes felt sore and he noticed the steel toecap of his right boot was exposed through chafed leather. The background traffic had ceased, the clock's ticking stifled in the torpid stillness; even the tomblike beds imparted the weight of sleep. He clipped the bare boards with his boot, just to hear a noise.

There was something he ought to have done today. Another appointment with someone forgotten? He felt a stab of guilt. Under the sad circumstances, in the blur of days it had slipped from sight.

He moved to the flat door and drew back its iron bolt. Smoke from pipe tobacco lay on the air, and he coughed. There it was again, stronger now. He turned quickly to the mezzanine, but couldn't see anything. It was too dark; even outside the street was in total blackness.

A cart rattled by, the sound of hooves and heavy crunch of wheels rolling over the stones. Someone began to shout outside, then more yells, and that pipe smell again. Was it a pipe or was it burning? His attention was summoned by a loud bang and furious knocking on the window.

Reluctantly he opened the shutters. A figure was flattened against the long glass, waving frantically, his face ashen against the night. Despite the urgent hammering, Ben found he was unhurried and slowly unbolted the door.

'A fire, Mr. Glee. A fire!' the man gasped. 'Come quick.'

But he was indifferent to the man's anguish, and looked beyond him to a tall, older figure.

Ben was afraid and knew he should not intervene with his business, and left the matter in his hands.

The acrid scent of smoke stung his nostrils. He stumbled back into the shop and slammed the door on the street's mayhem. Falling over beds and into furniture, he clawed at his private door and heaved his weight up the stairs, tearing at the bare boards.

The bedroom was illuminated as bright as day from

a blaze that filled the night sky. He tried to force the window open, but it wouldn't budge. Fumbling around for the catch, he slammed his fists against the splintered wood, prising his fingers beneath the frame.

Looking again, Ben saw his knuckles were bleeding on the plastic. He blinked in the pink from the setting sun. 'What shutters? Carts? Glancing at his feet, he tried to orient himself. No boots. Here? Where? 'I'm not part of this!' he shouted as he awoke.

On the opposite side of the road outside the hotel, Sophie was slouched on a bench looking very twenty-first century, a plastic cup in her hand. Behind her, the last of the day's bright caresses were withdrawing into February dusk.

Earlier that Same Day

The ticket office at the local station had taken up where the antiques dealer left off in the unexpected department. There was some confusion about the destination.

The ticket clerk, a man, who, in Prunella's blistering estimation had the charm of a bailiff and the expression of a thrashed backside, couldn't find the station.

'Not here,' he'd informed Sophie, staring stonily above her head, the only indication that their interaction was over.

When she'd pointed to the card and read out the name, the clerk had shoved out his bottom lip, eyes now feasting on her dismay. 'Nothing I can do. I can't invent a place, can I? Not my job to make things appear on my computer that don't exist.'

'What's the nearest one to it, then?' she'd enquired in desperation, before realising.

His was an irrepressible smirk, her dumbness to be savoured and no doubt destined for other clerks to enjoy. 'What happened to your old granny, then?' he asked, reaching for the blinds.

'That was ages ago. Will I be fined if I don't have a ticket?'

'Use the machine. See if it can find nowhere land,' he'd said, behind her reflection.

She did, and without any prejudgment it had offered up the station. When she'd checked the map, she found it was on there, too. A few stops from

Guildford. And her mind had carelessly plotted a humiliating end to the clerk's career. At least.

She'd arrived and, with purpose dispatched, she sipped at her coffee and gazed around.

The day had been eventful from the start – crammed with incident, as Granny would say, and Sophie felt the better for it. Even if the result of all that effort was just to close an account in a shop in town that, according to ticket men, did not exist.

Thinking about it, Glee's had been a very small, ordinary shop considering all the expensive beds it stored. It obviously went back a long way. Certainly further than she'd been able to see.

She placed her bag with the catalogue on the bench. This nowhere land was the kind of place that left you in peace, presumably because you were nowhere, too. And she felt quite at home sitting there and, without interruption, could probably have sat there thinking, a lot longer.

Ben, the manager, was walking across the road, and towards the bench. Not quite running, but in jerky uneven strides.

When he arrived beside her he looked very white and shaky. She watched his face carefully and waited for him to speak.

'I saw you sitting there. I was upstairs, and I saw you,' he repeated, a little out of breath and waving his hand in the direction of the shop. 'I wondered if you were okay. Not lost or anything?'

Perhaps he is, she thought. He does look kind of freaked out. It took a few seconds before she moved her carrier bag from the bench to let him sit.

He perched tentatively next to her, and said, 'Thanks. All a bit ragged, aren't we, one way or another?'

That was another surprise. Are we? she wondered. How would he know? I thought I was getting better.

'Are you just down for the day, Sophie? Sorry if I was rather short, earlier. I feel I was a bit rude.'

This Ben just appearing didn't make sense, and her thoughts were still lodged in his previous statement. 'Yeah. I'm getting neater and you're becoming scruffier.'

He quickly glanced down at his clothes. 'Am I? I meant, you know. Perhaps we've both had things happen and it's been a bit tough going.'

'It's like I've lost mine, even though she's still alive,' Sophie explained from her usual internal non sequitur script. 'My mum and me just don't get on. We hardly ever speak to each other. It shouldn't be like that. I've got no idea what she's going to say.'

His eyes darted over her in the way most people's did, If they were patient, they'd try to catch those random thoughts and place them in order of irrelevance. Most didn't bother.

It was unfair of her, the way she didn't bother to unscrabble her thoughts for others. Selfish, she realised that, and would try a little harder in future to make an effort. 'I know what you mean, Ben. I'm pretty lazy really. But you've probably worked hard and now you've got the same result, the same feeling. Nothingness.'

She felt his puzzlement rather than alarm.

He said, 'What do you do, Sophie?'

'How do you mean?'

'Work wise?'

'Nothing.' She grinned. 'Don't give me a job. I'd bankrupt you in a month.'

'I won't. I wasn't thinking of that. And actually, I'm quitting. Selling up.'

'The shop's yours?'

'The business is mine, yes. It's been in our family for centuries and I'm the last one. The last Glee standing, well, in this branch anyway.' He hadn't meant to make joke.

Sophie had accidentally kicked over her cup. Lukewarm coffee splashed over her legs and onto her feet. 'Because of your mum?' she said, ignoring the small puddle. 'My grandmother said you should never make a decision in a crisis. Or it might've been the other way round.'

He took a moment to process that. 'There's merit in either. She sounds as if you should try to like her. She lived all those years, after all.'

His eyes, as far as Sophie could see them in the growing dusk, were engrossed in something.

'What did your mother die of?'

She shouldn't have asked that so bluntly.

'I don't know. Confusion, I suppose.'

The town hall clock struck five. He said, 'It's a bit chilly here. I'll walk you down to the station. There's a train at twenty past.' He lifted her empty cup from the ground and placed it in a nearby bin.

Sophie got to her feet and scrunched her coat, feeling in her pocket for the ticket. Twenty minutes wasn't long enough to walk down to the station, especially if you had to cross over to the other platform.

'What time's the one after that?' she asked, noticing how tall he was and deciding she didn't want to rush.

'They're every half an hour. So fifty two past as far as I remember, unless they've changed the timetable.'

The sun had practically gone and the air nipped at her nose and fingers.

Ben walked fast, glancing around as if expecting someone. For a moment a cloud crossed his face as he strode beside her, and then it lifted.

She saw the wet laces of her trainers had come untied.

'This is very odd,' he admitted to her. 'I've never done anything like this, talking so openly to a stranger. Not that you are a complete stranger. You know what I mean. It's just not me. I hope you don't mind.'

'You did it on a whim,' she said, watching the words unfold on her breath. 'You don't have to explain everything all the time; things just happen.' It was said a little sharply for her. Like someone finding a clearing in a dense wood is startled by lances of light, she just needed to see things quickly before they disappeared again.

And he looked different, too, battered, fallen into his own natural softness. Not that she knew anything about him, apart from what he'd told her.

Her plastic bag was splitting from that heavy catalogue. She lifted it to her chest and secured her arms around it.

'Actually, talking of letting things happen, Ben. I've got myself into a bit of a pickle, whim wise. A total fucking mess, in fact. Sorry. The kind of mess a dippy, lonely cow gets herself into with a biological clock and a not very ordinary bank.'

A gulf in the flow of gentle chatter. She imagined his eyes widen, confounded by this unwarranted information. Dismissing. Registering. The concept.

'I only did it once. It's going to be what my grandmother would call no pedigree,' she said, almost to herself. 'On one side, anyway.'

She felt pursued by an unwanted stranger who would soon catch up and interrupt any new words left to save her.

'I don't suppose it matters which train I get,' she admitted, sadly. 'I don't think there's any actually going where I need to be.'

The road they walked fell silent but for the monotonous pounding of their feet. Ben vanished from her radar for a second or two, and she was alone.

'You only need the one,' he answered, with surprising ease. 'As for the other stuff, heredity is not everything.'

Which, for what Ben was about to do, was quite right.

Sophie didn't know that.

1857
Portsmouth

The Show Continues with Incident

Humphrey Purse, writer of plays, actor of melodrama and would-be impresario, rested in his stifling dressing room and peered into the looking glass. He was exhausted. It had been a good house, but the intensity of the evening's performance had strained every sense. Now, by the sheer mastery of that portrayal, his own soul felt under siege.

Despite the hammer and commotion of scenery being dismantled, the laughter from the small, private parties, he remained transfixed before the baleful portrait of his character – a reflection as distinct as another being.

Taking a wetted sponge from a jar, he began to mop away the poisonous powders, the dust stains and deceits of ageing. By degrees, as he peeled off the padded nose, removed the wig and rubbed out the pencil lines, a man of some thirty four years emerged.

The refined features were curiously avian. The long nose was sculpted from marble-white flesh, the eyes, now freed from their charcoal pockets, were a piercing blue and his head of thick silvering hair glittered beneath the smoky lamps.

Amid the busy array of pots and jars on his dressing table, lay a small ebony-framed portrait of his young actress wife. Tonight he was anxious to depart the theatre and return to their lodgings, where she waited for him with their infant boy.

They lodged in Twigmere, a small and pleasant town. Despite its gentle setting and good vistas, it was Humphrey's intention to move his family from the place as soon as it were possible.

He had been in dispute regarding their vermin-infested accommodation. The landlord, a shopkeeper called Horace Glee and his avaricious wife owned the leases on most lodgings in the town, and none of them decently kept.

The landlord, disgruntled by the complaint, was unable to offer a substitute of similar size at such short notice. But he had, begrudgingly, a smaller cottage at his disposal, newly vacated. The property was unfurnished but for the bed. Take it or leave it.

Humphrey had accepted, only to find the new lodgings were more ancient and decrepit than the original, with barely a grate and oven to keep the perishing rooms dry. Furthermore, Glee's son, Benjamin, a great brute himself, was sent to raise the rent on this ramshackle dwelling.

Determined to find satisfaction, Humphrey had visited the shop to demand Glee offer recompense in the form of goods.

They argued until, beaten by the actor's booming eloquence, the shopkeeper gave in.

'I be down on stock,' Glee had said bitterly, 'but will provide any at my cost, even though I will be the one to starve.'

With these events still vivid in his mind, Humphrey gathered his effects and dressed for the journey home. To amuse his wife, he included in his bag a variety of comic eyeglasses and a mask. It was the least he could to do for, since their son was born, she had missed her dancing, not to mention the applause.

The actor slipped from the stage door and into the teeming Portsmouth street. He drew up his beaver skin collar, took a firm grip on his leather bag, and walked briskly to the inn to take the London coach.

Stepping inside the carriage, he was assailed by the presence of a foul-smelling drunk slouched in the opposite corner.

The wretch sneered at him, and stretched out a filthy hand in greeting. The cuff above, though well-stitched, was ill-fitted. A thief, Humphrey decided. A leech waiting to feed from the lone traveller.

Purse gave a curt nod. A seasoned showman, he had both nerve and temper to deal with such menace. And if his courage failed, which it rarely did, the gift of invention and fakery was at his disposal. He gripped the silver top of his brand new walking stick, and considered the possibilities.

'Are you travelling all the way to London, sire?' the drunk enquired, his voice laden with mockery. 'I see you carry a fine case. Good leather. You be a doctor, sire? A potion within its satin lining to ease the liver, the fevers? I could do with easing.'

Purse affected deafness.

The creature drew nearer, inspecting his prey. 'We be companions for the long and dangerous journey.' He gave a splutter of laughter, baring what remained of his rotten teeth. 'But not as perilous as the sea, or ships what sail her.' Cheering himself on, he tugged out a bottle from his breeches and sloshed the rum into his gaping mouth. 'I been to Portsmouth to get rid of my obligations and what a pit of devils that place be. Admirals and whores, matlows blind with the pox. I don't have no woman,' he continued. 'Best gone, women, and I reckon you'll agree. Mine give up no money to bury her. How am I to feed her growing soppy son? You tell me that, sir.' He took another noisy slug of drink, and angled his face at Humphrey. 'Queer looking fella. Good at sniffing out the coins with that beak. But well fed and turned out, altogether, ain't you? You stick to me, Mr. Ambrose Bind. I'll see you right.'

Purse continued to stare grimly ahead, artfully working at his own bag and pockets.

Bind swayed, unseeing. 'And whoom,' he said, leering, 'do ay have the privilege of sharing the journey from that most salubrious town of Portsmouth with, may ay arsk? I take it the gentleman comes from abroad.' He slumped back, eyes black with intoxication. 'I sent my boy out there. The navy's got him now. Fifteen, he was. I done his papers good, and glad to get shot of the stinking little tyke.' He shook his pockets, rattling the coins. 'I got plenty and from better folk than you. More learning than a quack. You'll not meet a man more cunning than Ambrose Bind, you won't.'

All the while, Humphrey remained stock still, employing his subtle industry, discreetly easing out more from about his person. He'd done it many times and with mesmerising effect.

'My boy won't know it till he wakes,' Bind muttered, a moribund weight to his slur, 'too late for him, but I sleep with ease.' He sidled up, his stinking breath on Humphrey's cheek. 'Now you hand over that juicy bag of yours, full with its costly medicines and you can live to rob another patient.' A knife glinted in his hand, the other stretched out and about to cover the actor's mouth.

And still Humphrey did not flinch, impervious, as though encased in an armoury of steel.

The would-be thief drew back. He jolted away in fright, blinked and froze.

Purse moved his head a fraction. In a long grey wig and white mask, his reddened eyes like glowing coals, he imparted the hideous countenance of Death.

Bind began to shake, his grip loosening about the knife.

With aberrant, mechanical and hypnotic slowness, Purse turned and burned his merciless gaze into his assailant. 'I know you, Ambrose Bind! You are not long for this world,' he rasped with impressive force. 'For your many sins and cruelty, you are cursed from this day. You will never escape my haunting.'

Such was the power and conviction of his delivery that the wretch began hammering on the carriage ceiling. 'Stop!' he bellowed. 'It be the devil! Let me out!' he shrieked, imploring the coachman to stop.

Although they'd barely gone beyond Southsea, Bind threw himself from the carriage, receiving a thrashing from Humphrey's walking stick as he fell.

It was an enjoyable spectacle and a performance the actor was minded to visit upon the venal Messrs Glee.

After a brief conversation with the coachman to explain the pandemonium (a subtle warning in its telling for villains rarely act alone), Humphrey continued on his journey to Twigmere quite secure and unhindered.

March 2015
Twickenham

Sophie's Mum

A Late & Unexpected Appearance
&
Early Budding

Sophie sat upright on an orderly settee, the carpet vacuumed and a tray arranged on a small Chinese table. She had another visitor. This time, her guarded politeness suggested that it was the company of a total stranger.

'Where're you going to stay, Mum?'

'Not here,' came the brisk reply. 'I booked into that place in Richmond. Just two nights.'

Sophie's face flickered with relief. 'Oh.'

'Actually, you look quite well. Rested, in fact,' the mother observed, coolly. 'I am disappointed about the job, obviously. You can't expect to doss around for the rest of your life.'

'What's Edinburgh like?'

'Cold. Why?'

'Nothing.'

'How about using your degree, Sophie? Or has that gone past its sell-by date?'

The daughter was already exhausted.

Mother and daughter shared little resemblance. Sophie melancholic, the mother brittle. And at this moment, no evidence of affection existed between them. How these mismatched souls ever get thrown together is an eternal mystery.

The mum leaned back into the settee. She had Prunella's grey-blue eyes and her hair, once red, was now streaked with white. Her frown lifted. 'I'd forgotten that magnolia. Really livened the place up when it was in bloom.' She looked around. 'But it still looks like a student squat in here. You really ought to get rid of this lot, and that junk piled in the hallway. How's the drinking going?'

Sophie wanted to say it made her sick now. Instead she shifted her position and reached for a dry biscuit. 'What shall I do with her? You know, the ashes thing?'

'Whatever you like. I'm not taking them. Scotland did not figure in my mother's life, and neither did I.'

'Still feel the same then?'

'Of course. The old bat never considered anyone's feelings, but expected everyone else to accommodate hers. What's not to hate?'

'She's your mother. Was.'

'Hardly.' She rose from her seat and crossed to the window. A finger hovered at the sill, but resisted its critical trajectory. 'In fact, I'm not convinced your grandmother was actually human.'

'She was an eccentric,' Sophie suggested, deciding to accept a verdict of those months before.

'That conveniently covers a multitude of sins, including murder,' the mother said, peering through the filthy glass.

Sophie quickly dunked a biscuit in lukewarm tea. 'Well, she's gone now. And I've been thinking. Granny was just into her own thing. I mean, she wasn't actually wicked. She didn't mean to actually hurt you, or anyone.'

'Well, she did. And you've changed your tune. If damage begets damage, then we've certainly achieved that in our family. And do not forget your grandpa and way she dumped him. . . ' The mum broke off, catching the end of her train of thought. For the first time that day, she looked unsure, a wary eye on her offspring. 'I suppose you could resent me, the way things turned out.'

Sophie didn't answer.

'Will you sell?' the mother said, to fill the gap.

Sophie returned a puzzled look.

'Here. The flat.'

'I don't know. How do I know?' Sophie paused mid biscuit bite. 'You're okay with the will thing?'

'I'm fine, but I think she inherited as well. So at some point you'll need to find the title deeds. And I have no idea how you're coping with bills if you're not working.'

'Granny paid ahead for ages.'

'Did she now? What is it, the ghost that keeps on giving . . .?'

Sophie felt her stomach squeeze.

The mother coughed. 'Okay,' she said. 'Now I am here, I suppose we may as well sort out what to do with these ashes.'

In the bedroom, Sophie folded her arms. 'They're on there.' She nodded to the desk.

At the sight of the urn, the mum paled and directed her attention to the messy bed. 'I remember this bloody thing,' she said, quickly. 'Gave me nightmares. You don't sleep here, do you, with that thing?'

'Mum, can I tell you something?'

The mother wasn't listening, teetering on the edge of an unclaimed feeling. 'You've not fixed that window, I suppose. It never shut properly. Always like a bloody fridge in here because of that window.' She was at the wardrobe and flinging open the doors. 'It's empty. Christ's sake, Sophie, where are her bloody clothes?' Her voice veered from its taut hostility and tumbled into panic. 'You've got rid of them. You didn't tell me you'd already got rid of them.'

'You said you didn't mind. They're only in bags. You can have it all back. I don't care.'

'I don't want anything of hers You can keep the lot.'

'Then what's the matter?' Sophie watched as her mother stumbled over to the desk and loomed over the urn. 'Can you hear me? I don't want anything that belonged to you. I never did. I wish I'd never been born, and so did you.'

This time she really did feel sick. 'Mum. Please, Mummy. Don't.'

'Why not? What has she ever done for us? Look a this. It's not a home. How could a child live here?'

If the thought had been maturing in the daughter's brain, it now fell, audaciously ripened from her mouth. 'If it was that bad, Mum?'

Was that a question?

A shadow swiped the mum's face, knocking her expression inwards. She sagged down at the desk, pulling and closing random drawers. 'I do know. You don't think I know?' It was uttered more in righteousness than regret. 'Anyway, you were older.' Her face was shielded behind a curtain of hair. 'You had Dad then. It's not the same. And I wasn't mad.'

Sophie's voice was clear and unhindered. 'Exactly the same, actually. You went to live with Grandpa when you were small, and when I was little I stayed with Dad. When he couldn't take me anymore, I had Granny instead of you.'

What is there to say? These things only matter if people want to blame or to find an excuse to hide behind.

The mother folded her arms and levelled a blank stare at the window, an admission scarcely audible in her words. 'We used to fight. I even hit her once.'

Sophie sat on the bed, pricking the cover with her fingernails, her pulse cold and fast. 'She never said that. She never said that you hit her.'

'It didn't feel like real hitting. I didn't think I could hurt her. I doubt she even felt it.'

'How do you know? You don't know that. It doesn't always show.'

'She was never there, Sophie. Away with the fairies, as your dad used to say. I just couldn't find another way to affect her. To make her feel. What can a child do to make her mother feel?'

Sophie remained stony-faced and didn't say anything.

'Oh, now *my* daughter hates *me*.'

'Mum, you're the one doing the hating. I mean, it's not that bad.'

'Yes it is. Our lives screwed up. Look at yours. You're not exactly Miss Confident. Everybody's screwed up because of it.'

'Then make it better. Think it better.'

The mum's pride bolted from indignant eyes. 'I

really must try harder, mustn't I? Who do you think you are now, my bloody therapist?'

'Do you see a therapist? I thought about doing that.'

'For God's sake, Sophie.' But now the mum was out of her depth, and found she couldn't swim. 'We're behaving like children. Have you noticed, as a family? Look at us. We're like orphans. Bastards, in fact.' She had found Prunella's postcards on the desk and was manically shuffling them around, spreading them out in a fan, like a tarot reading. She leaned back, her arms limp by her side, mouth trembling.

Not sure what else to do, Sophie went over and gathered up the cards. They were mostly from art galleries, photographs of stately homes and grand houses, the backs smothered with Prunella's illegible gashes of black ink. Written to herself, perhaps?

'Look, Mum.'

But she seemed too terrified, and couldn't spare the glance.

Sophie abandoned the cards and lifted the black diary. She sat on the corner of the desk, and leafed through the empty pages to the March entry. Idling really, to see if she'd missed anything.

At last the mum looked. 'What's that?'

'Her old diary. Nothing in it. Just my birthday, except I wasn't born then. There's something in December . . . Oh, Mum. I'm sorry.' She hadn't noticed that before. 'Yours, Mum. I forgot.' She touched her arm. 'I totally forgot.'

'It doesn't matter. I probably forgot myself.'

The day faded around them, both women meditating on the space they each occupied, without and within. If they had gone as far as they could with talking, then that would be enough.

There had been no apology, you wouldn't expect it. As Prunella observed, 'Once the hounds catch the sorry scent they'll be tearing you apart for lifetimes.'

Yet that didn't mean to say she didn't have regret.

The window rattled and an icy breeze curled beneath the curtains. Sophie felt its grip on her wrist. She reached across and opened the damask onto that waiting light. Her eyes quickened to the garden, where pink tips of the magnolia tree reached to the deepening sky. Her mother would find out sooner or later, if she wanted to.

She stood, snapped back the window-catch and eased up the warped frame. The cold beyond was empty but for that almost naked tree. She placed her hands over the urn. Her fingers were pale and smooth, their grip firm. Determined. Unapologetic.

The mum looked across. Her face was frozen in an expression that was impossible to read. Recognition? Of what, the loss or the gain? Rising to her feet, she joined her daughter, her own hands supporting the rotten wood, fingers lightly touching.

Sophie caught her eye. No malice. Empty. Her history in it. An unprepared blankness that maybe needed help with something.

Sophie leaned forward and stretched beyond the sill. A sigh of wind, a crash, the thin roll of metal on concrete.

Ashes to ashes, dust to dust. Live, we try. Return, we must.

Mother and daughter quickly slammed down the window, trembling as if they had achieved the most momentous thing. The window catch bounced off.

Somewhen
Twigmere

Different Hat, Same Hands
&
The Mannered Part

Upstairs in the small cottage, Gifford Hans, attired in charcoal grey suit, high-collared shirt and purple cravat, pottered about shuffling paper and delving into filing cabinets. A meagre shaft of sunlight fired the stones set in the wrought-silver frames of his glasses.

After much rummaging, he gently eased out an old catalogue, the cover almost crumbling in his fingers. He blew away the cocoon of dust and cobwebs until the title was clear. *Sale of the Property of a Lady.*

Tottering downstairs, he settled in his chair and placed the catalogue on the low table. Delicately lifting the pages, he peered at each faded illustration until his eyes lighted on an entry: '*A Good French Bed with much Fine Decoration and Cartouche Carving of great Intricacy around the Headboard and similarly Carved on the Rails*', it read.

An invoice was attached to the document and held in place by a rusty staple, but the figures were impossible to read. He closed the catalogue.

He moved to the mantelpiece and picked up a letter lying there and read its contents with an expression of surprise. 'Another resignation.' Returning the envelope to the iron shelf, he took up the old wooden clock. It had stopped at just before quarter past eight.

Opening the front, he eased the hands back and returned the clock to its shelf. No sound of ticking, the face staying obdurately at three minutes before seven.

The old gentleman smiled and raised his palms in an attitude of gracious surrender, if not defeat.

He reached for his usual appurtenances and left the cottage, catalogues and miscellaneous papers abandoned to the falling dusk.

Strolling gently down the hill, he gave the railings a playful tap with his stick, drawing its tip across the iron bars, as a child would a xylophone.

He arrived at the busy junction of the main road in jaunty humour, stopping opposite Glee's bedding store. He watched two figures, a young man and woman, disappear in the direction of the railway station.

Earlier, the young man had strode purposefully up to the shop and stepped quickly inside, slamming the world behind him as one who is tired of its intrigue and pain.

Mr. Hans raised his eyes. The skies dimmed, streets emptied and still he remained at his vigil, opposite the shop's door.

Dawn's light slipped across the impromptu vista, hope, the quickening of a town's waking pulse, a winter's daybreak.

Customers, mostly female, came and went, the tinkle of the shop doorbell surprisingly clear.

Hans smiled as an expensively dressed woman tottered from the shop and over to a bench. When he joined her on the seat, she snatched up her large bag and turned her back to him. She soon vanished.

Hans sat, his eyes trained on the shop window and

its patterns of activity, darkness falling over each completed day. Morning sun followed by grey, deepening cloud drowned in inky night. Spring yielded, summer flowered, its leaves singed by autumn. Like a revolving stage, seasons came and went, the shifting scenery rolling ceaselessly about him.

Years passed, lives wound down, some ravaged by age, others strangely reborn. The shop's step deeper, windows taller and their glazing thicker.

A boy crept furtively from the door. Young Joseph kicked a pebble across the now deserted street, looked around and then bolted ahead.

In the distance, trailing years behind, carts replaced cars, gas now lit the windows, their radiance thinner, long skies crowded with ochre clouds. This time, a distinguished-looking gentleman departs the shop, an expression of concern burrowed in his handsome features. Second Benjamin Glee didn't see Mr. Hans, and strode up the hill, his boots dragging, foreboding weighted on each step.

The old man's gaze trailed after the figure until that, too, disappeared from view.

The place was deserted but for yet another man, another shopkeeper plodding towards him. This one a bewhiskered fellow, fumbled with his cap, straightened it on his head, his brow creased as if studying a worry. Behind him at the shop's upper window, the comfortably solid figure of a woman searched out. Struck from the warm amber light – a vignette of love and concern.

Hans smiled. Optimism ripened in the air and blossomed on hedges and in trees. Limbs looser, more nimble, he pulled to his feet, watching as Jacob made his journey up the hill.

The air became thinner, sharper, streetscapes hunched low and naked beneath a widening sky. The square, now void of memorial, was a dusty hollow, and a brand new hotel, its orange eyes sliced by shadows, slept.

Hans's expression tightened and he braced himself once more for the next appearance.

A heavily set character, a pipe clenched in his mouth, emerged from the shop and stood scowling by its awning. His manner was belligerent and fearful – both bullied and bully. Here was a conscience waiting to be pricked, or tricked. Hans chuckled to himself.

The shopkeeper, the first Benjamin Glee, folded his arms across his apron and surveyed the street, his dark eyes burning with suspicion. His attention was drawn to something a little distance away. Nodding his head, he pointed back to the half shuttered shop window. He began speaking as if in communion with an invisible presence.

'Excellent beginning and not badly played,' he acknowledges with a wicked smile. 'But only you, Mr. Glee, an ill read brute in poor sight could rename me thus.' Lifting his walking stick, he twirled it in the air and, giving a little bounce, spun on his heel. With a lightness to his step, he proceeded.

The day is starting again. Somewhere, some time, nearly at the beginning or the end. Somewhen, as they say on the Isle of Wight.

The name '*Glee's*' is newly painted above the shop's awning. Behind the shutters the shop is dressed with flowers and bright furnishings. A sign has been written on the gleaming window: '*Fine Continental Beds (& quality Mattress included). Perfection in the Discerning Lady's Boudoir. (With the conveniences of delivery and promise of quality or adjustments made at Glee's expense*), it declares.

The mattress turner rises to his full height, clicks his heels again and commences his own pilgrimage across to the railings and the start of the cobbled hill.

Halfway up, he's buffered by a strong and sudden wind and his hat is blown across the street. He chases it up and down the hill, until at last he pounces upon it with a furious yelp. 'Damn and blast you!'

He hears laughter and turns.

'Humphrey Purse, you shame me. Are you now the Grand Old Duke of York, with your halfway ups and halfway downs?'

A young woman is framed in the doorway of a small cottage. Her red hair is dressed with flowers and an emerald gown flows around her tiny form. Her face is too alive with mischief, the manner too capricious for her to be described as beautiful.

Despite her years, she is at least twenty four, her appearance conveys the restive impudence of a child. Yet her teasing seems to entrance the man and melts his temper.

He dusts down his hat, and presses his lips to the top of her head, and then gives a long kiss to her mouth. 'Would that be so bad, dear wife? It would keep us employed.'

She stands on tiptoe and rocks in his arms, stroking his face. 'Never mind that, Humphrey. You will not believe your eyes. Glee has played his tricks again.'

He ducks in the low doorway and is immediately in a small, miserable room. Even the wholesome smells of cooking fail to relieve the bleakness.

The place is so cold that the family have to sleep downstairs near the fire with their infant son.

Humphrey pushes past his wife and to a bed fitted tight and awkwardly in the room, forcing the rest of the furniture to exist in a triangular shape. He lifts the corner of the bedding, prods the mattress, bends and sniffs at it. 'What is this? All my wrangling for nothing! Who came?'

'The son, Benjamin. He was gone before I saw what was brought, Humphrey. If I'm left alone, how can I keep constant watch on everything. You know what a sly bully he is.'

Seeing her distress, he drops his effects on a chair, and cups her face between his hands. 'It's not your fault, my little Prune. There is nothing to be done tonight. Feed the boy now he's woken.' Lifting the infant from the bed, he hands the warm bundle to her.

It's bitterly cold, and while she nurses the baby, Humphrey builds up the fire. The coal from the bucket is almost gone and he uses the old bellows to draw the flame.

When the child is fed and returned to the covers, his wife prepares the table for supper. Two crystal glasses and a jug of wine sit on the lace cloth, embroidered napkins in silver rings are set at each place, for every precious night the family spend together is a celebration. She brings over the bowls of hot broth from the tiny stove, and soon their faces glow, their tempers soothed and wicked landlords momentarily forgot.

The baby sleeps soundly. Husband and wife eat and drink, talking and laughing softly, their heads bowed, fingertips touching.

The dishes can wait till morning. She takes his hand and guides him to the bed, where they stand watching their son.

Humphrey stoops near, and listens to the tiny snores. 'He likes it. Regardless, he does sleep well.'

'And it should be in a bed from the Queen's chamber, not this pit.'

'Do I have a rival in high circles?'

'Only a mother has the certainty,' she teases.

He prods the mattress once more. 'This is well used and filthy. Those infernal villains have escaped too long. We'll think of a new way to deal with them. I'll give them another show.'

'I hear of your performances,' she jokes, a gentle tug at his ears. 'Giles Overreach, next time, or perhaps a Faustus with that face.'

'I fancy Mephistopheles himself,' he says with some seriousness.

'Be careful with the look. The wind could change, Humphrey, and I'll be missed down those long centuries.'

'Then I'll bring my sour plum with me.'

'Sour? A woman must always make the sacrifice. I may as well be dead as stay buried in this place.'

At this, Humphrey sidles to his bag, slips out a pair of the comic spectacles, and balances them on his nose. 'What is death but another stage on which spectres parade,' he proclaims.

'And what is acting? You must find out else we all will starve.'

Laughing, he bundles her into his arms, ruffling her hair. 'And what about the jeers for you?' he hisses at her ear.

'You are mistaking your own. They worshipped me,' she replies and grabs the spectacles.

'And won't this worshipping husband satisfy?' Humphrey lifts her and spins around. She pretends to escape from his clutches and they wobble and fall laughing to what little floor is left to take them. She curves into his arms and they stay entwined, their faces pressed close.

After they dress for bed, Humphrey lights the oil lamp and sets it carefully on a small table.

She eases up the child and folds back the covers, resting him in the middle. 'The sheets are freshly done,' she whispers to her husband, 'but who knows what else nests in here. We may find eggs for breakfast.'

Humphrey cluck-clucks softly, and follows her as she slips into the bed, both careful not to disturb the child.

He stays near the lamp and reaches for her hand and squeezes, their arms a shivering bridge across their boy.

The house creaks and groans, unwinding from the day.

'Humphrey,' she murmurs from the surface of her dreams. 'This mattress is old tick, and alive. It does need a shake.'

'I will shake Glee and within an inch of his life,' he whispers and rolls over to turn off the lamp.

The last of the fire's dying embers wink at him like devil's eyes. 'The name of Glee will be damned until their lot are mended in their ways.'

'You'll wait an eternity for that. An itch never to be scratched.'

And then Humphrey remembers, and laughs out loud.

'Shhh. What now?'

'A felon on the London coach. Went by the name of Bind. I'll show you how I paid him back.'

'Not now, dear husband. We have all tomorrow for your games.'

'And all the perfect rest, my beloved Mrs. Purse,' he promises her slumbering head, his own thoughts already scattering in sleep.

The infant's tiny breath, light and pure as a white feather, rises and falls as he sleeps between his parents.

A spark, the window rattles, carelessly abandoned clothes, a bed too near a hearth. Whosoever fault can match the scene the moments are perfected for endless night.

The smouldering of straw and leaves. Smoke, a shroud that binds the nostrils and chokes the lungs. The falling curtain of suffocating darkness surely spares them at the end? One prays so.

The speed of fire, cloth and timber. Gone are dreams, tricks and vanities. Their stage stretches, an empty and impossible conceit.

The play is dead. Long live the players.

Now Happens All the Time
Twigmere

Benjamin Goes Fourth?
&
The Rest

Idling from the station, a traveller soon discovers the treachery of country roads. Taking their life into their hands, they'll dash across to the opposite side, before a speeding vehicle sweeps around the bend and sends them to kingdom come.

Once the perils of single pavement roads are safely traversed, their efforts are rewarded by its verdant edges, the trees shouldering the wide sky, the air that infuses the lungs with health and vigour.

As they proceed, the visitor to these sylvan parts will be enchanted by the row of quaint cottages clenching a small hill, their spirits will soar at the hanging tiles in muted pink, blinking at a bruisy sky.

Trotting along with a heart light as a balloon, the visitor soon arrives at a junction. Nothing discordant here, no clumsy planning disasters, the road yields organically into a natural and heartfelt curve.

A memorial to those who fought in the two world wars stands in the centre of a wide thoroughfare. The column rises from a triangle of green, surrounded by borders of well tended flowers. A bench has been thoughtfully set beside, its seat now dappled in an autumn sun.

On the opposite side of the road, a decent hotel

offers lunches, including discounts for the elderly.

Sprouting from the surprisingly busy high street, little lanes bloom with specialist shops. AGA outlets and a well-respected store are among their welcome surprises. The local charity shops are well-stocked, top-end cast-offs piled high on laden shelves. And, borne upon Twigmere's sweetly fragrant air is that nascent thrill, the magic rub, the ghost of jumble sales past and future.

For the dealer who likes to fight and rummage, to get one over on the competition, these places offer a frisson to warm the blowy, country days. Yet for this traveller, this antique dealer down from the hard-faced metropolis (Putney, no less), it is not the plundering of innocence, the unguarded treasure troves that bring them to this delightful Surrey manor. For once, it could be said, she seeks something far more elusive than stock.

After lunching at the hotel, she steps onto the street and wonders why she'd missed it. There it is. Glee's Bedding, right before her eyes. Except that today its windows are forsaken and stare blindly out.

Glancing up, our hunter dealer reads the For Sale sign and moans quietly to herself. She peers through the window and into the recesses of the shop, her eyes straining. She can just make out bed frames, then she has in her febrile sights the muscular contours of something familiar and fantastic. 'Is that it?' she wonders.

A door, not spotted at first, is opened at the back. Shapes break and reform, fluctuating in the dense grey. 'Is that him? The man himself?' She flicks back an unruly strand of hair.

The woman stoops low, squeezes her eye to the letterbox, without noticing that her purse, hanging from a gold chain, has fallen open and dangles to the ground.

She hears something. Talking. Voices, young and old, but can't be sure. Even taking a step back, she's unable to get a good view of Glee's to see what's going on.

On the other side of the road, at the foot of a small hill, she watches lights go on and off in the flat above the shop. Silhouettes passing back and forth. There is definitely someone there. It may be worth a try.

The dealer fumbles in her purse. Her glasses are missing. In a moment, she's back across the empty road and retrieving them from the stone step, along with a small burgundy card, also escaped from her clutches.

The woman yanks up the shop door's stiff old bronze letter flap and slams it down hard as she can. Again.

Her rapping continues, determined, persistent and echoing. Like the rest, forever unanswered in that sleeping street. In a town too perfect to be real.